Run, River

Run, River

Sue Webb

Matador
9 Priory Business Park,
Wistow Road, Kibworth Beauchamp,
Leicestershire. LE8 0RX
Tel: 0116 279 2299
Email: books@troubador.co.uk
Web: www.troubador.co.uk/matador
Twitter: @matadorbooks

ISBN 978 1800460 324

British Library Cataloguing in Publication Data.
A catalogue record for this book is available from the British Library.

Printed and bound in the UK by TJ Books Limited, Padstow, Cornwall
Typeset in 11pt Cambria by Troubador Publishing Ltd, Leicester, UK

Matador is an imprint of Troubador Publishing Ltd

For Nick

PROLOGUE

I have seen the Mississippi. That is muddy water.
I have seen the St Lawrence. That is crystal water.
But the Thames is liquid history.

John Burns, MP (1858-1943)

The river runs outside the world.

A lot of it, at least. Of course the doomy estuarine vastness beyond the city holds little scope for lands of fantasy. It would be a perverse voyage of pleasure that took you down past Ebbsfleet and Gravesend, towards Ham Ooze and Black Grounds, Mucking and Foul Ness.

But inland, where the river might be Isis as much as Thames and glints along by reedy eyots and cornfields fringed with willows, there the spirit unbuttons itself. That much our three anti-heroes did know from the start. At ease in reflected summertime light, the psyche straightens up and blinks in the sun, smiles at nothing much, then seeks salvation through harmless acts of folly. Some people go and build waterside gazebos all of glass with, say, an actual stuffed hippopotamus standing where it can best overlook the seasons and the boats. Or spend money they didn't think they had, on a thatched roof where straw herons keep company with the real thing or a fox made of reeds might stalk a matching pheasant.

Others, dawdling down the river in a punt with a folding canopy and bedrolls, or atop a fibreglass monstrosity whose engine could power a frigate, seek the Neverworld night under canvas of some half-forgotten children's adventure book. On a damp Oxfordshire islet they wake to a sunrise like the world's first morning. Or it would be, if they hadn't been so drunk that now there's a great scorched hole in the tent, after some idiot said the experience wouldn't be complete without naked lamplight.

The river runs with history as well as innocent illusion. What kind is down to you, whether a legend, brutish and faint, with Saxon warhorses up to their fetlocks in blood, or a scholarly glimpse of court life, all inventories, head lice and heavy silks. Many people go all out for medieval-themed banqueting, where the vegetarian pizza option is named for a beheaded Tudor queen and the troubadours wear sneakers. And some can never see a particular Augustan palace without an X-ray notion of what exists beneath, knowing that under a marble floor built for the elegant geometry of cotillions and gavottes there lies the heaped chaos of a plague pit.

The more history, the more beginnings. Even free spirits who despise harking back can take heart from tales of revolution fearlessly enforced. Vainglorious Papist tombstones have been rooted up for useful bits of road, and medieval stained-glass angels beaten to a slush. In former centuries the river's very sources, long revered, became sacred no more as Church reformation reduced the Blessed Virgin's Well to Black Mary's Hole.

Who says you can't change the world? Some people claim there've been times when men of the future could see off history itself.

I

Now, the clustered roofs, and piles of buildings trembling with the working of engines, and dimly resounding with their shriek and throbbing; the tall chimneys vomiting forth a black vapour... the clank of hammers beating upon iron, the roar of busy streets and noisy crowds ...until all the various sounds blended into one and none was distinguishable for itself...

The Old Curiosity Shop, Charles Dickens, 1841

Eliot, driving south to their rendezvous.

How could any landscape be so bricked over, yet feel so remote?

The Bentley surged over dead railway cuttings full of buddleia and Japanese knotweed, and past closely mown deserts of fouled grass where factories had stood, but now used only by the occasional dog-walker. Amid demolished streets a lonesome pub had boarded windows and a sign with a faint crude likeness of Queen Victoria. Mainline railway gantries strode to the horizon, heavy and dark like felt-pen graffiti against the sky; nearby a ten-acre car park winked in the bleary sun.

The factory chimney was the thing he noticed, glancing up from his work in the back of the chauffeur-driven car. As old smokestacks went, it wasn't much; but throughout this decaying vista no other landmark stood proud. And you couldn't miss the square billboard on top. It was set carefully askew, as if balanced by one corner on the nose of a circus animal. 'Leave It All With Us', it read. Seen in the middle distance the chimney seemed to fluctuate in height as buildings nearer the motorway rushed by.

The storage company's name could also be glimpsed, forty feet high on a scarlet pre-fab wall. Most of what Eliot had owned was indeed boxed up and stashed with them. Out of his sight for ever, since his business partner had unexpectedly declared himself bankrupt. After the first rush of dismay, Eliot had scrabbled everywhere for funds of his own to rescue the company: a boardroom equivalent of looking under the sofa cushions for lost change. Some of his possessions could be got back; but the motor would have to be downgraded, and the agency signed off that supplied its drivers.

Now that his business had been salvaged, he was relieved to find he'd lost almost nothing that he'd miss. His private life had seen so much uprooting that shedding nearly everything had long since lost the power to knock him down. He'd been divorced three times so far, to no one's surprise but his own. What could you expect, people said, from an idealist like him? The type who thought that if you had a girlfriend – to whom, say, you'd just finished

introducing your friends – the next thing you were
supposed to do was marry her.

True, his mishaps mostly sprang from optimism. But
the same undisciplined hopefulness had lifted Eliot out
of trouble far more often than it dropped him straight
in it. His company did holidays, for a loyal and growing
clientele who in another age would have been travellers,
not tourists. On the Silk Road or in the antique gardens
of Mughal India few of them would have cared about
going a fortnight without a shower; but at every point they
expected serious scholarship, from the best people there
were. He'd founded and run the business with unthinking
obsession, like a garden-shed astronomer oblivious of
his own efforts in the thrill of finding an unknown star.
People mistook him at first, seeing only a genial man
who, as one ex-wife put it, resembled every child's most
treasured stuffed toy. But in the world of work he showed
an instinct for detail as tight as a gin-trap. Formal clear-
mindedness, as well as too much trust: both had their
effect on his small, long-serving workforce. Faint-hearts
and skivers might think to take advantage; good workers,
women especially, knocked themselves out for him.

In the back of the motor, Eliot was working down a
list of calls.

'Not according to article 10 of the 1986 Act,' he was
saying. 'You need to look at the provisions made in the
1994 Order; also, as I said, at *Investment and Pensions
Advisory Service Ltd v. Pantling …*'

Most of us have more than one voice, depending on
who we're with. Right now Eliot spoke in the tone of a

good-humoured man who on this one issue, then this, was nonetheless immovable. Anybody overhearing might think he was all pinstriped up like some corporate Angel of Death; in fact he wore a sweatshirt and jeans, fraying at every hem and put on in childlike impatience for his imminent holiday to start. Already at the back of his mind was the slip road by which he meant to have finished up and shut off the phone for the rest of the month.

He just hoped he needn't give up the boat. That would be a different order of loss, for reasons that had nothing to do with money. For years it had been yearned for, then never used while building the business went on consuming his nights and days. But the crisis in his affairs had left Eliot seized by a spirit of, If not now, when? So today at her mooring in the Cotswolds, the *Speedwell*, an antique cabin cruiser updated at never mind what expense, was waiting, newly serviced and ready for any adventure he and his friends had promised themselves.

Meanwhile it was hard to believe the boat was only a county away. The car swooshed through a crypt of concrete pillars, where an intersection stood three levels high. Or there would have been swooshes, except that the world outside was silent when seen from a motor as grand as this. One subtopian vista followed another like a montage of scenes from a wraparound silent movie. A dead-car mountain rose sixty feet high, chewed into a scree of fragments. Arc lights towered over marshalling yards whose boundaries were lost to acres of birch scrub. A terraced street, slate roofs, angry-red brick, had been cut across by the throughway, leaving former neighbours three miles apart the short way round. Along one horizon there loomed what looked like a baleful cloud formation, pale grey and perfectly flat on top; a second glance revealed it as the half-kilometre wall of another warehouse, owned by a company based up the Yangtze in a megalopolis that hadn't existed a decade ago. Dwarfed against its blankness, a blackened Victorian church rose up in front of it like a piece of street art.

The only vivid thing for miles was a narrow boat in scarlet and cobalt blue, on a sepia canal with litter-fouled banks. Crewed by tourists perhaps, who'd missed the way to Shakespeare country. The landscape swooped to and fro around the unrolling motorway: at one moment a factory built flush with a stretch of overpass showed its rooftop one yard above the throughway parapet; elsewhere a signboard gantry framed a vista of tower blocks like giants caught in mid-stride. Then the struts of an empty gasholder towered straight ahead. In clear weather, through its frame you could see an azure smudge signifying far-off spacious pastures and steep beech woods, like an unattainable idea of themselves. But today was muggy, with such things visible only to the gaze of the imagination.

How he hoped, nearing the bottom of his list, that this was the last call he'd make to his soon-to-be-ex business partner. Bernard wasn't a bad bloke, however much Eliot currently disliked talking to him. He'd merely accepted the wrong job. Eliot, conscious of not having been to university, had been overly impressed by Bernard's academic background. Too late he'd realized that the well-respected authorship of such titles as – if he remembered aright – *Stochastic Factor Analysis*, or *Latent Variable Consolidations via the Biggs Clumping Heuristic* – was no basis for a career as a finance director. Worse, Bernard's command of economic theory didn't even help with his personal life. Snared in household debt, he'd furtively borrowed from the company. Setting the law on him would have been futile; besides, Eliot felt it was partly his own fault, for having misjudged the man. Accordingly he'd put himself out, as now, to help him, amid talk of bailiffs' cursory levies, notices of distress, walking possession agreements, exemptions from seizure, and all the other glum jargon of being up to your nostrils in toxic debt.

Exchanging a careful 'Well, good luck, Bernard,' and a 'You too,' each dour with embarrassment, at length they rang off.

That left one incoming message.

'Hello, Eliot.' Marina's throaty voice was warm, like savouring some vintage with a good finish. As ever though, all he heard was suppressed anxiety. She only called when willing herself to ask a favour.

His first ex-wife's history of self-invention was formidable; nowadays he had trouble perceiving her as a solid reality. For half a lifetime she'd slogged away at re-jigging everything about herself – appearance, history, the lot. Before she went to secretarial college there'd been no such person as Marina. Eliot was probably the last person left who knew her baptismal name was Mary Ann.

There'd been a time when he'd thought her life a blithe venture through one possibility after another, as if looting a dressing-up box for grown-ups. But being married to Marina soon felt more like watching a general as he clapped on a frown of purpose, the better to invade Russia out of season. There flickered through his mind the half-remembered fact of a procedure described as a hand-lift. Didn't it involve transferring fat from the buttocks? And wasn't that just the sort of thing she'd be due for, about now? As her life's latest doggedly achieved milestone?

'…I thought I'd call now because I knew you wouldn't want to hear from people later on…'

'People' meant two persons: Marina, and her son Roland, the upshot from one of her two disastrous later marriages and a not necessarily employed twenty-eight.

'…I expect you'll want to be incommunicado, won't you, on the boat…?'

Eliot knew why she'd called. This was Marina as impoverished but loyal parent, seeking advancement for her child.

'…I know I've been in touch already. Well, you know, left another message. But …now that your business needs a replacement, you know, for, um, Bernard … well, Roly's experience in finance would make him ideal – that is to say, not necessarily the perfect appointment – obviously one could never say a thing like that about anyone with total certainty – but he would surely be at least ideal as a candidate. I mean, you know, if you do have a shortlist. Anyway, I won't keep you at a time like this. What I mean is, I don't want to disturb you when you're on holiday…'

A slave to the idea of herself saying the right thing, Marina had remembered to add, 'Do give my love to your friends – to Mike and Chris. I know we haven't met for years; but, well, you know …'

There was a pause at her end, as if she were paying attention elsewhere. With the knowledge given even to the most guileless ex-spouse, Eliot clocked that Marina was not alone. It didn't take much to picture her, turning to look anxiously up at someone as she added, 'Oh – and if there are any new developments after all, then of course you'll be able to get Roly on his mobile phone. Any time, night or day. It'll be no problem for him … And, well, I appreciate that you owe us nothing after, you know, what passed between us all those years ago now. But, anyway … Bye …'

Eliot put away the phone. With heart-lifting suddenness he saw that they were leaving the conurbation behind, and were now among the coppices and pillowy fields of Worcestershire. The city's last grungy pre-war suburb, ranged on its green horizon like a leeward line of foul weather, was sinking from sight, and the southern range of hills cradling the headwaters of the Thames had advanced from a wistful idea of themselves, to become almost real.

I I

Let me not to the marriage of true minds
Admit impediment; love is not love
Which alters when it alteration finds …

Sonnet 116, William Shakespeare

Chris, riding east.

Around the time Eliot's grand motor reached the rust-belt part of his journey, it had been passed in the opposite direction by a car belonging to another member of the *Speedwell*'s crew.

Chris Lovell, Eliot's friend for twenty years and his sometime colleague, was due to meet him at a rendezvous a few miles short of the boat. On a hilltop above Cheltenham, his wife Martha had already dropped him off; from there she and their teenage son Tom were about to drive north to see her parents in York.

In Russia, when people were about to part, traditionally they sat together for a minute or so in silence.

'I think that would be a bit effusive for us,' Martha had remarked, as she and Chris were getting ready to say their goodbyes. She had a line in quiet irony that flourished nicely alongside her husband's forthrightness, a trait of his that strangers often mistook for cynicism.

'But a ritual like that could still be useful,' he'd said. 'For families pretending they cared. When in fact they'd got nothing to say.'

They'd parked near a grassy bluff with benches set facing a view across to the Welsh mountains, and were about to mark their own farewell with a flask of coffee. As Chris closed the boot his phone rang. He went to take the call perched awkwardly half in and half out of the car.

'No one enlivening, then,' murmured Martha, unpacking some plastic mugs. 'If it's somebody who cheers you up, he usually walks about while he chats.'

'I bet you it's Imogen,' Tom said. 'Even if you can't hear what Dad's saying, you can still tell.'

They glanced back at the car.

' … So when did Daddy die …?'

The voice of Imogen, Chris's cousin and foster-sister, sounded faint, as if a distance of three or four dozen miles was all that modern electronics could cope with. When saints claimed to hear far-off celestial voices, even they must have sensed contact with something more forthright than this.

'…Can you tell me, Chris?'

Not for the first time, Imogen left him blindsided. Had her mother – had anyone – really not told her at the time that her father was dead. And if so, why?

'It would have been, oh, just under a couple of months

ago. He died on the twentieth of April,' he added, mindful that the smallest uncertainty was supposed to worsen her condition.

'Oh.' At twenty-six Imogen still sounded more child than woman. He imagined her gaze, unfocused by concentration as she made the effort to talk. 'Mummy thought I'd better not go to the funeral. She said I'd be too upset.'

As so often on the phone to his cousin the line went unpredictably quiet. Chris was preparing to fill the silence with something harmless, when she added, 'But she did explain. When she left the house to go to the funeral. She did say it was because Daddy had died.'

He felt a small, queasy adjustment to reality, like finding you'd hurt yourself at blind man's buff. So...Imogen hadn't been told, when her father died? Obstinately loyal to both his foster-parents, he suppressed any feeling of surprise, much less censure. For God's sake, he told himself: who else could have known what to do, better than Leonora? Imogen's mother was an agony aunt, a powerful presence in more than one public medium.

In the matter-of-fact voice you used with Imogen, he said, 'I'm sorry I wasn't there either.' Chris had been in Iceland on a dig, and various failures of communication had kept him there until too late after his uncle's sudden heart attack.

He added, 'I owe him more than I can say.' He meant it all the more as a man who guarded his feelings. Chris had been an adolescent when his own parents had perished within the same year, each from a different hard but commonplace smoker's death. Thereafter he'd been brought up by Imogen's parents, in an atmosphere of all-enveloping friendliness. The mystery was that only one child out of two – Chris, the half-grown lad cruelly orphaned – had thrived. With a conscientious mother and an indulgent father, how was it that life had left Imogen's inward self so bruised?

She said, 'Are you writing your speech about Daddy?' At his uncle's memorial service in London a few days hence, Chris was one of several people due to climb into the pulpit and address a grand gathering at St Martin's in the Fields.

'Yes, I am,' he said. 'I'm going to work on it while I'm on holiday.' Somehow you ended up talking to Imogen as if you too weren't quite normal, laying out your words like high-stakes playing cards.

'And you won't mention me, will you?'

Again he found himself caught short. No wonder her mother, invincibly self-possessed in public, was privately stricken at Imogen's retreat into the shadowy far depths of self.

And who would have thought pure pity could be such a gobsmacker? At work Chris was thought of as omnicompetent; at academic conferences and in committees, smiling but serious, he seemed able to carry any argument. But with his injured-fledgling cousin, even he was hard pushed to say the right thing.

Not one memory of her as an infant had hinted at baleful things to come; two-year-old Imogen had shone with glee just to be alive. Foremost among his recollections was her discovery that soap bubbles cast a shadow made up of colours. She'd laughed so delightedly, she pissed herself.

He replied, kindly as he could, 'I'll do whatever you like.'

No response. He never knew if her silences were down to medication, or institutionalized loneliness. Thank God there'd always be everything for her that money, at least, would achieve. He and her mother, as executors of Uncle Hugh's will, could see to that.

He signed off as best he could, having passed the phone to the others so that they could each say hello and goodbye: Martha in the tone of wary encouragement she used in Psychiatric Outpatients, and Tom conscious that his 'not-dead-yet-then?' approach mightn't be quite the thing.

Martha uncapped the coffee and started to pour it. 'Where's Leonora in all this?' She passed her husband a cup, gauging him with a look. 'I do think she can be a bit brisk with Imogen. Not the way she'd be with any of her public.'

Chris sipped his coffee, frowning at this as mightily as Justice obsessing with her scales. Martha had known he'd respond like this, even as she'd failed to stop herself.

'I can't believe you really think that.' His voice was mild but inflexible, in a way no one beyond his family ever heard. 'She and my uncle spared nothing when they fostered me. If you'd been there, at least then you'd understand.'

Carefully Martha said, 'I can't imagine them treating

you any other way. Just as I can't imagine you being ungrateful.' She knew she'd touched on the one subject that vanquished his usual self, humane and sceptical.

Above the huge view across the Severn into Monmouthshire they sat and drank without speaking, then made the effort to talk of indifferent things, till Tom judged he could add, 'Anyway, Dad, whatever's really wrong with Imogen, you're just too nice to figure out the rank underbelly of the human heart.' He'd recently got a taste for mixed metaphors, which he wielded without mercy.

'Yes, but you only said that because you liked the sound of it.'

With more such half-serious sparring they finished up, unloaded Chris's bike, and got ready to leave. He and Martha tended to avoid shows of affection in public. As usual though, he couldn't help putting his arms around her, to savour unthinkingly how slim she was. And Tom, tall or not, he embraced as one would a child of any age, albeit in response to, 'Goodbye, antique Dad.'

Chris knew he was lucky in his everyday life, and had the sense to remind himself often of his good fortune. Freewheeling eastwards to join his friends, under a fine-weather sky feathered with mare's-tail clouds, he did so now, as any good and grateful man should.

I I I

...and so to [Whitehall] bowling greene and up to the top of the new banqueting – house there over the Thames, which was as pleasant a place as any I could have got. And all the show consisted chiefly in the number of boats and barges – and two Pageants, one of a King and another of a Queene, with her maydes of honour sitting at her feet very prettily... Anon came the King and Queene in a barge under a Canopy, with 10000 barges ... And so they landed at Whitehall bridge, and the great guns on the other side went off.

Diary, 23 August 1662, Samuel Pepys

Mike, heading west.

The houseboat had been listing, as it did twice a day. Its mooring beside a communal floating walkway showed up on Google Earth as trendy beyond belief. Down at water level though, the boatyard's disorder was at best picturesque. A previous owner with a self-mocking take on retirement had named the boat *Dun Fawr*, perhaps

15

mindful how, so near the riverbank, it was forever at the mercy of low tide.

On board this wasn't usually a problem. Things tended to stay where they should, on bunks or in overhead cupboards with sliding doors. There had been one undeniable mishap, when on the higher, landward side a drawer had slid open that held Bianca's newest underwear, all that froth of lace-trimmed stuff she'd bought for their honeymoon. No problem there, except that Mike had left a bedtime mug of water on the surface above. From ten feet down the boat he'd noticed too late as it ambled to the edge, then neatly tipped itself upside down among his wife's most prized silk chemises and bustier. It hadn't helped her mood that, instead of embracing her right away and consoling her with his usual ardour, at first he'd just sat down and laughed until he had to wipe his eyes.

Not much flustered Mike. Small accidents just enlivened his day, and even the larger shoals and rapids of existence left him unafraid. The fact was that so far in his life every decision had come promptly. Even under sniper fire in Bosnia his men had known that Major Caldicott would cope without a heartbeat's hesitation.

For a man so resolute in making the best of everything, the only pressure that might faze him was living under other people's control. It wasn't through his choice that they were housed on the boat; it belonged to a friend of a friend, who'd wanted a tenant for a few months. And Bianca in any case would have needed somewhere to live. For she too was recently divorced.

So much the better that the four of them – they and Bianca's two-year-old twin daughters – could start their life together somewhere different from the ordinariness of yesteryear. What could be timelier than a change like this, away from his sensationless world of two-car garages and pet insurance, not to mention her life of extended family where engraved napkin rings were used at every meal? The view from the boat was wonderful: not at all suburban, but bounded up-river and down by trees and large gardens. At night, when the dining area was reconfigured to make a double bed, they could drift towards sleep in one another's arms while semi-conscious of the river flowing or eddying around where they lay.

These were the waters, he would murmur woozily, down which the funeral barge of Good Queen Bess, England's Gloriana, had voyaged in pomp from Richmond to London; likewise the massive pageant of gilded barges, of banners and waterborne musicks, bearing Catherine of Braganza downriver to become Charles II's Queen. Mike normally had no feeling for history, as a tone-deaf man might say that music was doubtless fine for some people. Yet now he insisted to his new wife how it was only fitting for two people like them to find themselves in such an interesting place.

Too bad that Bianca was usually asleep by then. If not, she still wouldn't have known to marvel at such retro stuff when uttered by a man determined to free himself from his own personal history.

This morning was their first parting. En route to Lechlade, to join 'those friends of yours – the ones who laughed a lot', he was driving Bianca to Heathrow. She was taking the twins home for a fortnight to Lisbon, the better for their progress in potty-training and sleeping to be admired by her many aunts and cousins. Given how much he and Bianca would miss each other, he was surprised to feel a disillusioning moment of relief once they'd all been got into the overloaded car and the boatyard entrance was receding in his rear-view mirror. What of all those memories they'd garnered there so far, right down to the first time he'd bumped his head when stepping into the galley?

But no, their present life of travelling light had only one real drawback. When he'd happily agreed to be housed on the boat – for a nominal rent, mates' rates – it had been temporarily moored somewhere else. Under the Westway, in fact, where the massive one-note vibration from passing traffic left the surface of the canal permanently blurred. Since this had only been a short-term address, Mike was genuinely tempted to laugh at what he called the oddity of their situation. He felt bad, though, that Bianca somehow hadn't see the joke – a fact that left him more relieved than he'd admit when with an exclamation of 'Westward ho! Yea, to Brentford and beyond!' he'd cast off and driven the boat to its present mooring.

Their new location did have one surprise drawback. Not that he minded, so long as Bianca wasn't upset. Almost as reliable as low tide, at certain times of day a shadow fell across them. Only literally, of course. And no one had planned it this way: neither the boat's owner, nor Mike, nor Anna herself. But there she was, his ex-wife,

newly moved in just before they'd taken possession of the
boat, with a tenth-floor balcony view of them from only
a quarter mile away. In another century the site had been
noisy and fouled, occupied by a tannery and glue factory;
now the new apartment building where Anna lived was all
shining wood-block floors and kitchens with fitted granite
counters. The flat must have been bought – Anna must
have bought it – for the view, over the woods and ponds of
Richmond Park and beyond to the North Downs.

Also – here Mike couldn't resist feeling just a bit good
about his own generosity of spirit – why should she move
away from where she'd put down deep roots? This had
never been a part of town where people who were young
and poor churned through in crowded flat-shares. Say
what you would about the over-furnished world from
which Mike considered he'd broken free, with its residents'
associations and state-of-the-art security systems, its
tennis-club memberships and lawnmowers with a driver's
seat. But if other people – if Anna – preferred life that way,
well, why not?

Actually Bianca had taken the fact of her predecessor
as a neighbour very well; you could almost say she'd
looked demure. And no one could claim there'd been a
show of bad blood between him and his ex, even during
the divorce. He could tell that she too must surely think
their long marriage had successfully run its course,
from the efficient way she'd set about selling their house
and generally settling up. The lawyers' correspondence
– the only communication there was – had been free of
recriminations or strife, and Anna herself, no doubt from

tact, had retired for the duration to her brother's house in Brighton.

Not that he would have dreamed of showing her any disrespect, had they met. He'd prided himself on dealing fairly with both women. In Lisbon, following a fortnight at a conference with the IT firm for whom he now worked, it became borne in upon him that no self-respecting man could have entered on a relationship like his with Bianca, then just bolt. Back in London he'd written Anna a letter asking for the dissolution of their marriage in terms of such deathless gratitude for times past that certain phrases still reassured him of his own perfect gallantry. No man should speak ill of someone to whom he'd once been married. It just wasn't on...

On the motorway to Heathrow this morning the car was almost warping with family life, like an organ strained by the workings of an arrhythmic pulse. True, Mike himself had cut free from all former ties, and was now the very image of a man living life off-piste. But most of Bianca's recent past was still right here: little Maria and little Claudia, thankfully both fed and rested enough at this hour to regard screaming and shitting merely as options to be held in reserve; also a mountain of luggage, much of it child-related, including ready-made-up bottles of feed, a sterilizer unit, and nappy packs the size of hay bales.

Least ignorable of all, because so violently happy and grateful to be there, was Monty, the retired sniffer dog bought by Bianca some months ago to be a playmate for the twins when they were older. He was mostly a large spaniel, with floppy ears and a tail proudly borne that wagged with unstinted commitment to good fellowship. Cars delighted him – as how could they not, since much of his working life must have been spent scampering in and out of them, quivering with self-fulfilment as he sought and presumably found all sorts of sinister stuff. He's probably got more medals than me, thought Mike with the faintest inward sigh as Monty cavorted and delved amongst the luggage piled in the rear compartment.

Silently preparing for their scene of farewell, on the motorway they were assailed by only one crisis. Amid flat cabbage fields and monolithic airport hotels, and beneath a flight-path sky roofed with standing thunder, he was alerted by a yelp from Bianca as she looked over her shoulder.

Neither small child was showing symptoms of insurrection. Instead the crisis of the moment lay right at the back, behind the dog-proof grill.

No wonder Monty had taken early retirement from public service. Waggle-tailed Stakhanovite work-junky and upright citizen though he be, on journeys this length he did have one lonesome failing. He was car sick.

I V

…But, oh, how one toils against the inconstancy of the seasons & the elements in this place! When first I placed myself to paint this scene the infant river tumbled at the full, greenish, almost dark malachite in places, indigo where larger shadows fell, with glints of amber at the rim in fortunate lights. But the sun has shone so steadily that now the water is sunk to expose the banks, which are brown & ruined by winter, and so utterly counter to what I intended. Making good what I have done thus far has taken extra time, so that where I had painted the sun setting beside the outline of an elm, now it disobliges by going down behind some haystacks, which are grouped like monstrous rock cakes. A small crab-apple tree nearby, which I had started to show leafless, came into flower, & had to be clipped naked again by my faithful Esmeralda, standing on a hay bale loaned — so grudgingly! — by the farmer.

And tonight there is a halo round the moon, which must surely betoken bad weather...

Letter of 25 June 1916 from Edith Hart to her confidant and
younger brother Edwin (1891-1916)

A steep lane led up beyond the slip road. Dry-stone walls began to replace hedgerows, and the horizons grew wide and vague. Eliot the besieged businessman and ex-husband was surging free from his own history, to be replaced with what he saw as his real self: Eliot the scholar. For years sustaining his business had eaten him alive. Only at unnatural hours had he scavenged any free time, strenuously self-improving as any Victorian clerk who'd ruined his eyes by candlelight in some mean lodging where you could see your breath.

An Open University degree was the main handhold by which he'd hauled himself this far. Now he was researching a doctoral thesis, on his semi-famous great-great aunt Edith, an artist whose career at first had brought her little more than an early death from overwork and self-neglect. Thereafter she'd had a modest reputation as a painter of Thames valley landscapes, elm-shaded and evanescent, though still scarcely a footnote in other people's biographies, including her near-contemporary Stanley Spencer, with whom she'd had a pitifully ill-judged affair. Now, however, fashionable reappraisal was overtaking her. According to one recent exhibition catalogue she should be seen as 'an anti-sexist standard-bearer, in her life, her loves and her labours; and as an iconic figure of feminist resistance to tradition.'

'Bollocks,' had been Eliot's scholarly response. Already he felt the seeping wrath of the researcher who hadn't expected to find others – not to mention their clichés – on his terrain. Aunt Edith's life and works were exclusively his, dammit. And though by the time he was born she'd been dead for decades, secretly he saw this cherished project as an exploration of his own personal history.

Hence his detour down minor roads, even as the boat awaited him, with the big motor easing its way along dog-leg lanes between drifts of cow parsley. He was on his way to see the old stone house built on the site of a ruined nunnery, where Edith had foregone food, sleep and unsoiled stockings in the compulsive outpouring of several among her finest works. She and a group of other idealist women who'd 'chosen not to marry' had retreated here to spend their allowances on a quest for creativity and plain living, bringing with them two servants who privately detested the place and cursed its lack of modern Edwardian amenities. The house had already been verging on dereliction and stood in a valley once so remote that when Henry VIII's commissioners came to take possession of the place, the few nuns they found spoke only a half-perished form of Norman French.

In a lay-by on a breezy summit Eliot asked Charlie, his driver, to pull over and swap places. First though on getting out, he scrambled across the roadside verge to go behind a hawthorn bush for a pee, and celebrate his sense of liberation by expelling a shining arc of former breakfast-meeting coffee. He was halfway through finding how many kinds of insect he could drown, when a large chalkhill blue flitted into range. Seeing that this was the holiday's first upland butterfly, he decided to salute its appearance by sparing it, and soused a line of ants instead.

Back in the car, changing down and gliding on, he wondered when, on a day like this, could you say the holiday properly began? Was it when you turned off your phone? Or was it when easing up the slip road, away from the motorway in its universe of one continuous non-place? Would it be when the three of them met up in the pub by the mooring? Or cast off on the boat? Maybe right now was the defining moment of liberation: getting behind the wheel, the better to take in the sunlit morning and the motor's smooth handling.

The road crested an oceanic swell of hayfields skimmed by swallows, with views the breadth of a county. A shallow scoop of land turned with imperceptible suddenness into a combe with a tiny brook, then a narrow valley with a profile of beechwoods on each side descending in a glissando from the skyline. The driver of a dirt-encrusted Land Rover with a trailer full of sheep stared at them in passing; so too a woman in overalls and baseball cap, on a tractor pulling a bailing machine. On empty byroads the Bentley always got looks; more so here, as people tried to figure out a grungily sweat-shirted chauffeur in pudgy middle age plus the be-suited young black guy sitting behind him and concentrating with unassailable purpose on a thick scuffed textbook. Charlie was doing a postgraduate conversion course in law, and brought to it a steady, focused attention usually seen in police interview rooms where the outcome could only be serious.

Closing on Edith's former home, Eliot began recognizing themes and places he'd only known through her works. She'd been a watercolourist, trained in Paris. Her paintings were more readable than many canvases by Turner, but she'd been almost as repetitious as Monet in her quest for this hue of shadow or that shimmer of suspended damp. So, he thought: some places really did look the way she showed them.

Not quite watching the road, in this handmade landscape of sudden views, he met with a blip of illusion. Two riderless bicycles seemed to be running along the top of a dry-stone wall. Then a turn in the road showed them fastened upright to the roof of an approaching car. A flock of sports cyclists swooped after, legs muscled to the point of caricature, like a medical diagram. Half a minute later, in his mirror Eliot nearly failed to see another cyclist appearing behind him as if from nowhere. It was Chris, turning into the road from a narrow lane between crumbling limestone walls.

Eliot made an emergency stop and lowered his window.

'You're late!'

'I am not! You're early.' They'd been due to meet at Foxcombe End, Edith's home within the nunnery ruins.

'Why there?' Eliot had typed, on the bulletin board they shared with Mike when the holiday was being planned. 'I could easily meet you and Martha at a service station.'

'That won't do, thanks all the same. Foxcombe's near the source. And I fancy doing the whole river, not just the bit big enough to float your gin palace.'

'The Thames doesn't start in this valley. It says so in the guide book.'

'In the sight of God it does,' Chris had typed back. 'Bugger the book. You bought the wrong one, that's all.'

Chris stowed his rucksack and bike; then, introductions completed, the glass partition was closed on Charlie's implacable advance through Blackstone, and they drove on.

Chris said, 'Which part of auntie's life are you checking on today? Old Edith, or when she was young?'

'About to pop off. Around our age. Forty-two.'

'When did forty-two last have anything to do with you? Your teeth have got fillings older than that.'

'An almost Edwardian forty-two. Makes you and me look not too bad.'

Foxcombe End stood at the top of a once-metalled lane turned into a slough by cement-mixers and trucks. Until recently the site had been a lost domain, dismally neglected. But now a heritage organisation was in charge. Voices and drilling could be heard, scaffolding clad the largest remaining fragment of the church, and the muddy nave was an improvised car park.

They left the heavy motor a quarter mile short to avoid more of the churned-up track. While Charlie sat and read on like some implacable Muse – a personification of Duty, or Knowledge, or maybe just Not Being Done Down – Eliot and Chris made their way up the combe through damp grass starred with ox-eye daisies and red campion, past where an earthmover was deepening the shapes left by a stairway of ancient carp ponds. They were greeted by the site manager, who'd been one of Chris's senior colleagues until last year, when he'd found that a university life of research and teaching paid only half as well as this kind of work.

Amid much catching up on academic gossip he gave them a tour. The east wall's blind arcading and the broken socket of a huge rose window would be left unrestored, though like everything else they'd be buffed up, till they almost resembled a pretend ruin newly built to make the most of Upcote Wood as a backdrop.

The house itself had been built with stone looted from the nunnery, and stood inside a corner of the roofless church. Once repaired it would feature every modern comfort, unlike the frugal lamp-lit commune that Edith had known. It was here that the little settlement of high-minded ladies, professing atheists all, had set out to labour at their art or craft with the rigour and self-denial of the first inhabitants. The nuns had risen in the dark at all seasons for Lauds; six daily services later they'd attended Compline before retiring to their chilly cells to sleep like corpses.

Chris and the former associate professor were soon deep in debate on the merits for old masonry of hydrated lime mortar versus hydraulic lime. Eliot wandered off, through shaggy pasture and building-site debris, to take notes in the form of a hundred or more snapshots. Far more than he needed; but it was part of his nature to be anxious in his researches. He'd been leading a compartmentalized life, in which the confident businessman and the would-be scholar failed to know each other. Even now he was self-conscious at having missed out on university life. His friends might chide him for it, with Mike in particular calling him a silly sod. But the feeling persisted even in middle age, like a minor birth defect stoically borne from the first and never quite forgotten. He still had to remind himself not to look awestruck around various people – like, say, Charlie, who'd just taken a first at the LSE.

The site manager went back to work, and they accepted an offer of tea and biscuits, consumed while sitting in the sun on a fallen block of stone with a crumbling egg-and-dart frieze up one side. In the usual gabby way of friends going on holiday there was much to be said, as if they'd only got minutes rather than days.

'Is it all right,' Chris enquired in due course, 'if I ask about work?' He'd sometimes freelanced for Eliot's firm, as a supervisor of working-holiday digs. It was the kind of job, all broken fingernails, sunburn and proper scholarship, that Eliot himself greatly coveted.

'Of course,' said Eliot, though some skulking part of him guessed what Chris would ask next.

'So, this Roland chap. How well do you know him?'

'There's every chance he'll be perfectly fine.' It was hard not to blurt, in the face of Chris being calm and attentive. Eliot couldn't help adding, 'He's even family. Well, more or less.'

'Yes, I remember Marina.'

Eliot cast a look at Chris, trying to see what that was supposed to mean. To change the subject he said, 'And, uh, is it okay if I ask you about the funeral?'

'No problem.' Chris frowned, thinking of Imogen's

absence when her father was buried. 'Everything's fine. The memorial service will be too.' He described the speech he had to write, like a difficult holiday task, to be completed by the time they got back off the boat.

'The daft thing is, it's not as if I won't mean every word. You knew him –'

'Uncle Hugh? For as long as I've known you.'

'But how do you sound believable, talking up someone who's just left you a few mil?'

'Dunno. Ask Mike. Nothing gives him pause.'

'Right … Though maybe he should learn to dither sometimes. If he weren't so damn decisive, perhaps he wouldn't have bound himself over to this new woman.'

'Are we supposed to ask after her?'

'We can't not.'

'But what about the rest of his, um, family history?'

'Yeah… Martha and I both like Anna. Always have done.'

'You say "like", not "liked".'

'We still see her a lot. Like Martha says, she's such good company. Not like, um…'

'The new one. Bit of a bugger, trying to look enthused on her account.'

'Better let Mike raise the subject.'

'In his own time …'

'Well, I'm damned if I want to probe the poor sod.'

Once they were back in the motor, the valley slid by until the sky grew large again, and the stream swelled into a little river. The pubs stopped having upland names such as the Shepherd and Dog or the Woolpack, and were called things like the Wharf or the Ferry Inn.

Or indeed the Trout, where as arranged they found the boat, moored and ready.

V

Yes, friend, this is what I came out to see; this many-gabled old house built by the simple country-folk of the long-past times, regardless of all the turmoil that was going on in cities and courts...

Kelmscott Manor, described by William Morris (1834-96)

[Kelmscott is] the doziest clump of old beehives...

Dante Gabriel Rossetti (1829-82)

'Start as we mean to go on,' said Chris, indicating the pub, which appeared to come as a set with an ancient packhorse bridge. He and Eliot stepped out with purpose: an ignorant onlooker might think they were tackling an unavoidable chore.

On professional grounds Charlie had refused a drink – Eliot half suspected him of being teetotal; indeed, of knowing in medical terms what each unit did to a first-class brain – and had got back behind the wheel of the Bentley.

'Maybe I'll drive you again,' he'd said to Eliot, shaking hands with them in farewell.

'Represent me in court, more like, if I go bust and start looting collection boxes.'

'People with talents like yours don't starve,' Charlie had replied, with the authority of someone already robed up as a court Recorder. '…That's very good of you,' he'd added, surprised, as Eliot handed over an envelope with a murmur of, 'Something towards next Michaelmas term.' Just how much of the next year would now be sorted, gave Charlie serious pause when, back in the motor, he opened the envelope. For some moments afterwards, anyone who knew him might have been astonished by how little self-possession he showed.

*

Inside the pub, Mike was already there, ordering at the bar. There followed the low-key greetings of oldest friends, in which cheery murmurs of 'What ho, old man!' and other self-parodies belied their real pleasure in each other's company.

A round was got in, and a move made into the noontide sunlight and shade of the pub garden. Monty, tethered to a table leg, got up and wagged his tail as if greeting each one of them in the role of dutiful host.

The first pint was entered upon in ceremonial silence, before news and plans began to be swapped. Mike had come resolved not to hold forth too much about his new married life. So he was impressed as all hell with his own restraint at saying nothing before asked about it by Eliot, just as each was lifting his pint for round two's primary slurp.

'Actually,' he said, 'we're hoping to start a family soon.' He looked at his friends as if expecting a reflection, mirror bright, of his own swelling excitement.

Eliot, hell-bent on loyalty to the ideal of friendship, said, 'That's ...'

Chris was concerned merely to show respect by being bullshit free. 'I have to say,' he ventured, 'I salute your commitment to the future ...'

Mike sensed nothing of his friends' wariness. His old self could scan the social currents of a mess party as clearly as he'd learned to see each picturesque Balkan valley in terms of likely ambush sites and lines of fire. But now he was eighteen again, innocent and self-absorbed. His friends said nothing more; and briefly they all drank deep in silence, while at the garden's edge, with the waters shooting sparks of light, the nowhere-near-grown-up Thames went sauntering sweetly by.

*

On board the *Speedwell* for the first time, Chris's response was to sit down and laugh till he had to blow his nose.

'You use a remote for that!'

The galley could have held the gadgetry of their boyhood's science fiction. Dan Dare went right beyond the moon in a high-tech cabin like this. The *Speedwell* wasn't just a well-furbished craft; more a small transport hub.

Three folding bikes were stashed on the broad flat roof, and, as though she'd whelped, she had her own dinghy.

Chris had to take back what he'd said when he called her a gin palace.

'This isn't a rich parvenue among boats. You misled us.'

For, whatever digitised new freakery had been magicked into her interior, the *Speedwell* herself, all buffed-up brasswork, mahogany and teak, was an aristocrat among vintage motor launches, imperishably elegant like a silver-haired dowager outshining her own diamonds.

Despite the boat's splendours, modern and antique, tonight Eliot's cabin was going unused. The river offers everyone his own stream of other-consciousness; it embodies freedom, each man doing what he alone prefers. Eliot's first aim on their voyage was to wake on the roof before sunrise, in search of a particular Aunt Edith riverine effect of early-summertime first light. It was somewhere close by this mooring, in 1918, that Edith had sought the perfect setting to her majestic *Confluence: Fowler the Bargee as Witness to the Marriage of the River Gods Condatis and Isis near Lechlade.* This was a late work, mostly an effusion of light within which the figures were small and mysterious and a distant Thames barge looked frail as a blown leaf. Throughout a week of daybreaks she'd set up her easel and sat waiting, with a layer of *Manchester Guardians* tied around her for warmth under a filthy old motoring dustcoat. She was sustained by an early breakfast of bread-and-dripping sandwiches and sweet tea, prepared in pre-dawn darkness by 'our loyal Esmeralda, who's been with the family since anyone can remember. Donkey's years.'

Aunt Edith's work had seemed at first entirely of its time. But the more Eliot gazed and probed, the further her preoccupations led him on. Like him, she'd looked to history for a sense of self. In the letters and diaries, and in notes on work in progress, two of her ancestors had got particular mention. Will Fowler, known in his day as the Bargee Poet of Isleworth, had been taken up by royalty, when the court of James I inhabited the late-medieval palace of Whitehall as a waterfront town in its own right. With such patronage, plus the reputation of a plebeian prodigy, he'd gone on to write ten volumes of competent mainstream verse, including Odes celebrating the inaugural river processions for three of London's Lord Mayors.

Fowler's great-great-grandson Augustus 'Plenitude' Figg also had a nose for certain fashions. But though many of Figg's verses can still be seen, inscribed *in memoriam* on finest Purbeck marble, these were not what set him up with his coach and pair plus a riverside villa near Chiswick. He was a stonemason's son, made genteel by a career sculpting lush funereal monuments in the highest Baroque, from whose extravagant swags and cartouches he got his nickname. In an age of enlightened self-confidence his grandee clients took it for granted that he was the fellow to represent them at the last, each leaning against a classical urn or some such in their best wig, as if death itself were just another social obligation. 'Plenitude' Figg's Palladian villa, like an elegant dolls' house beside its great shadowy cedar, is depicted in the background of

Edith's *Dedingham Meadows: Queen's Reach at Sunrise,* where objects seem to exist not in themselves, but merely reflecting a birth-of-the-world blast of light.

'Do you think my reading list has missed anything?'

Eliot's need to be acknowledged as a 'real' student was an area where Chris trod carefully.

'Well,' he lied, 'it's not entirely my period. But I'd be flattered if you'd let me take a look.'

As expected, the contents page of Eliot's iPad, listing all he meant to read for his doctorate, was a marvel. Chris wondered if he should say, 'That seems to cover it,' then settled like a true and honest man for, 'Bloody hell!' His imagination faltered before a mental picture of all those monograms, letters, articles, notebooks, palimpsests, bibliographies, diaries and riverlogues piled together into something the size of a haycock, like a paper-based dropping from the bowel of a baling machine.

'That's the same as reading one book per mile.'

'You know perfectly well it's just an electronic comfort blanket.' Eliot came close to a blush, as usual when trying to hide his envy of someone else's scholarship.

Apart from his uncle's projected eulogy, Chris wouldn't expand upon any holiday task he himself might have, cherished or not.

'I'm just working on something of my own. Maybe it won't fail as tremendously as the last one.' A few months ago, moonlighting, he'd been hired as a writer by a film company. A documentary, thought his friends; but since they'd heard nothing more it seemed they'd better not ask further.

Mike, coming aboard, had plonked a rucksack on his bunk and got straight back off. He was soon out of sight downriver, sculling strenuously in the *Speedwell*'s dinghy and relieved to be breaking a sweat. Hard exercise came to him as a liberation. Some years had passed since he'd resigned his commission; but he was still straight and lean in a way that made civilian clothes look as if his uniform had just gone missing and he was making do till he got it back. Physically, compared to him both his friends looked like sluggards, even though Chris, elbow to elbow with his son, had easily finished that year's London Marathon. Running twenty-six miles was less trouble, he'd told Martha, than having Tom, ever the concerned child, satirize him as host creature to a paunch.

Pulling down the river, Mike was in reflective mode as he calculated his allotted distance for the day. Since the divorce, he figured there was nothing he'd missed except his rowing machine. The houseboat near Twickenham only had room for it on the roof; but Bianca had let it be understood that she thought he looked like a silly man up there, setting his face upstream while heaving away on top of a forty-foot vessel that went nowhere. The debate that followed had almost brought them to their first quarrel.

Love never comes cheap, he'd told himself, and her, immediately afterwards while holding Bianca as if to protect her from some physical menace. Self-respect kept him back from saying anything as clichéd as, what didn't kill it would make it stronger.

Their courtship had had every appearance of high romance. For one thing, it had stolen upon them in a foreign

38

country. They'd met at a conference near her native Lisbon, on the role of information technology in higher education. Mike found himself with a group there that increasingly included Bianca, who had an administrative role to do with the interpreters. They were housed in a former palace whose grounds had been planted by an eighteenth-century English nobleman gifted with fabulous taste, and wealth to match. From its hanging gardens and secretive paths through unbounded-seeming woods, glimpses of sea and sky suggested a single outer sphere of blue as if the whole pleasance were airborne and floating. The milord's grand terraces were bowered in arbours and overarched by lofty trees like a grand operatic set ready dressed. Realized, as they came to feel, just for the two of them as a mis-en-scene around their discovery of one another.

He'd never stooped to tell war stories before; it wouldn't have occurred to him. But Bianca's open-faced admiration deserved the fullest response he could lay before her, as she asked, 'But when you were a soldier, you couldn't have been afraid. Not as the leader of all those other men.' In conscience, not one episode of doubt nor choking dread could be withheld from any creature who heard him out with such focused wonderment. Every word he spoke was a debt repaid to her admiration, one that he was honoured to utter.

Marriage was nowhere in his thoughts, at first. Whatever possibilities lay spooled in Bianca's mind as she faced the return to what remained of her life in London, and a future as a single parent, Mike had acted merely as a child of the moment.

Then, after a few days of this addictive novelty, the emotional landscape changed, as she in turn confided the worst of her present life. She hadn't mentioned that she'd been divorced; now every withers-wringing detail came forth.

Of all the harshness and humbug with which her husband showed how much he hated her, so that putting her down at every chance was central to his sense of self, one especial splat of squalor stood out. He, an Englishman teaching philosophy at the university where she'd studied, had signalled her dismissal as his wife with a text on her phone. She was to give way, so she found in due course, to 'the only woman I could ever have truly loved': one Cressida, scriptwriter and matchless talent.

For a few blank seconds of staring at the screen the vindictive economy of her husband's first line had left Bianca mystified.

'U', it read, 'RX'.

For any big-hearted man, Mike thought on hearing this, such behaviour deserved only one response. The woman who had suffered these insults had a fineness of judgement and a generous spirit that had been obvious from the start. It had showed itself in how she'd looked up at him, gravely understanding, as she heard his own story. Now too she stood forth, modestly self-revealing, as an innocent wronged and in distress. Any absconding husband, even were there reason for divorce, should have explained himself to her with more respect and gallantry than that poltroon.

He knew he could have. In such a situation …

And now, as if summoned into sight by memory alone,

here beyond a small, tight bend in the river was a scene from their honeymoon. They'd prised themselves from their four-poster just in time for lunch in the hotel bar of the Ram at Burford, a building with a grand exterior of Carolean sash windows but an inside all made of timbered medieval crannies. Reaching the Thames on a chill spring afternoon, they'd toured the manor house at Kelmscott, where William Morris had sought to embody his dream of a yeomanlike Englishness and where Mike now showed his bride around as if he himself were the curator of each fine, plain room. Amid the panelling and tapestries there was one wall hanging, so he declared, that deserved an especial significance for them both.

In *Sancta Bianca in Her Bower*, the saint was sinuous as the interwoven living branches about her. She was all in white with a chaplet of daisies around her smooth brow, and stood in an arbour formed from a pomegranate tree. A grassy foreground at her feet was daintily tufted with windflowers, wild orchids, and white violets. On one side a swan lowered its head in homage; on the other, a white hart did likewise, tethered by a golden chain.

Mike had stood rapt before this image, as he saw it, of his new wife's inner self. At such a sacramental moment he'd been caught out however, by a disloyal shudder of relief that none of her massed relatives were there. The wedding had been the first time he'd met most of Bianca's family. In such circumstances there were bound to be surprises. Her mother – recently widowed, so maybe excuses should be made – had seen their special day largely as an occasion to shame the bride's delinquent ex.

'And when she married him, do you know, we all thought how the English were supposed to be such dependable men.'

Some might have thought Bianca's grandmother had a more tactful take on things – though it was still a mercy that her accent and laboured delivery only just left her intelligible.

'You,' she told the groom, with his gift for looking serious no matter what, 'are our dearest girl's white knight. After what happened to her and her babies, we prayed very often for a good man who could rescue her.'

At such moments the shortcomings of her relatives only endeared Bianca to him the more. She'd heard all this, with perfect tact and eyes demurely cast down. To him no other woman in the world, standing fast in the face of undeserved embarrassment, could have been so honourably forbearing.

VI

Interviewer: *And now, as part of our commemoration of the post-Impressionist painter Edith Hart, who died twenty years ago this week, it is my pleasure to introduce a guest whose knowledge of Miss Hart and her working life was both intimate and unique.*

Mrs Esmeralda Hodge was one of the Hart family's household staff for several decades, in circumstances offering an unparalleled opportunity to witness the struggles and hard-won triumphs of this remarkable and, some say, underappreciated artist. Mrs Hodge: when did you first become aware of Miss Hart's remarkable talent? ...Her talent ... Yes. As a painter.

Esmeralda: *Oh... yes, that. I suppose she was always at it.*

Interviewer: *You mean, from childhood?*

Esmeralda: *That's right.*

Interviewer: *Er, yes, well ... I believe among her contemporaries she had a reputation for frugal*

living and quite extraordinarily hard work.
As, for example at the commune, if I may call it
that, where she stayed for several months in the
Cotswolds? ... At Foxcombe End...?

Esmeralda: Oh, you mean that old house out the
back of beyond. Worst place I ever lived.

Interviewer: Miss Hart and her fellow artists
presumably saw it as an exercise in plain living
and high thinking?

Esmeralda: I couldn't say what any of them saw
in it. What I do know is, there was only two of us
to do the things that had to be done every day,
and no electricity nor running water. And they
never thought of a man, to do the heavy work.

Interviewer: Yes ... uh... But did you ever think
Edith Hart's choice of lifestyle found some form of
reflection in her work...?

Esmeralda: Oh, I wouldn't know about that ...

BBC Third Programme, 21 March 1949

On the roof of the boat before dawn the call of scholarship
had put an ache into every muscle of his body. Eliot had
set the alarm clock with precision, knowing to the minute
what gradations of waning darkness he sought on that
particular morning of the year in order to see what Aunt
Edith had seen.

'You sure about this?' Chris had said – then checked

himself before Eliot's purposeful glower.

This close to the bridge and the pub, the *Speedwell* had been moored in a line of other vessels. Eliot was damned if he'd face the awkwardness of waking other people with his alarm sounding off; so it had spent the night as close to him as could be, the two of them cosied together in the sleeping bag ready for him alone to hear it. Throughout a meagre few hours of sleep made scantier by anticipation, sometimes it had nudged him in the kidneys; at others it mimicked the primary symptoms of appendicitis by applying its hardest edge to his paunch.

At least he'd been awake when intended; no falling asleep just as he should have been rising to full awareness. But first light suggested nothing of the super-subtle palette deployed by Edith on this riverbank nearly a century ago. Here he was, expecting a radiant morning to fade up, like the visage of a naiad coming into view, when it seemed all he'd get was some ageing drab behind a veil the colour of apathy.

Then the alarm went off.

Well, okay.

Only then did he recall what an over-sophisticated toy it was. Voice-activated, no less. If, that is, you wanted it to silence it. First he sat upright in his sleeping bag, holding it close and whispering, misting it with his breath as if making a furtive phone call in the face of supreme danger.

'Shush,' he murmured. 'Yes! No! Shush!'

It beeped on, as addicted to duty as Monty himself when sensing an especially momentous whiff. Eliot retreated deep into the sleeping bag and again commanded the device to shut up, in a low but imperious voice that made up in urgency what it lacked in decibels. Then he tried closing the top of the bag over his head and growled out loud at the thing in the suffocating dark. Still he was assailed by failure.

Emerging onto the dew-soaked roof, rumpled in body and spirit alike, he failed to notice that rosy-fingered Thursday morning had advanced to where the horizon downriver was no longer a dark cut-out. The foreground held shapes too, soon to be seen as a herd of reclining cows and a ragged line of pollard willows.

Leaving the alarm zipped into the bag would bring no relief; the stupid thing was too shrill. In this motionless landscape, still scarcely three-dimensional, the next loudest noise was the splash of a moorhen taking off along the river's surface. Shouting was clearly not on, even if Eliot hadn't been too self-conscious to raise his voice.

Meanwhile the first hints of shadow had appeared and the sky's eastern rim was turning faintest green. What had just been obscurity now showed itself as a world of suspended damp made gauzy by the strengthening light, so that the line of moored boats seemed to float unsupported by anything but air. Whatever he'd come to see would soon have gone.

Eliot tore off one of his socks and thrust the alarm into it. With the action of a shot-putter, he circled, whirling the sock over his head at first steadily, then faster, with grim and sincere abandon. Dizzy though he soon became, he could still see clearly enough to hurl the thing into a neighbouring field rather than the Thames. It bounced insignificantly off the vast flank of a contemplative-looking Friesian and landed in a half-dried cowpat, now audible only to the nearby cattle, one of whom would silence it twelve minutes later with an arbitrary and thunderous moo.

At the moment of letting go, Eliot's feet shot from under him on the wet roof. Lucky for him that the *Speedwell* was, as Chris had remarked, an essay in creamy consumerism. A smaller vessel would have shrugged him into the river with a colossal splosh like a melted glacial cliff, hands and feet thrust upwards at the morning star. As it was, the boat resounded like a drum as he smacked prone on top of it, then laboured up and exclaimed something that could have been heard all the way over the water in Wiltshire.

His friends' questing faces shortly appeared above the edge of the roof. But Eliot was too distracted at that moment to notice them. How could he not have seen by now that the slowly lightening sky and water had taken on the tenderest hues of daybreak. A quarter mile away a row of black poplars, with narrow trunks half the height of a cathedral, were duplicated by their own reflections in the slow-moving water. At this hour, when the land had yet to gain full colour or depth of shadow, their tall silhouettes seemed unconnected to anything.

A moment from the beginnings of existence. So Edith did get it right. As if he hadn't known.

*

There seemed no point in anyone rolling back into their bunk. An heroic fry-up was substituted for more sleep, black pudding and Cumberland sausage not omitted, and the *Speedwell* cast off, with everyone's eyes screwed up against the early sunlight, that still glittered with mist. An anticipatory silence was observed as they sallied out for the first time into the river; its surface rippled beneath their bow with the lush sound of a long-awaited drink being poured. Monty, totally up for the role of mascot, stood in the bows, ears flapping, his silky tail held high like a banner of war and his flaring wet nose strained forward into the breeze.

As the day cleared and lightened, shapes in the near landscape gained definition; others, more distant, also shifted into view. The spire of Lechlade church, at first some miles astern, sidled this way and that with the river's windings, until at one point it seemed to rise among the meadows full ahead. Blearily seated at the wheel, Eliot felt mindful of what his other semi-famous ancestor, Will the Bargee Poet, had had to say of the river's benign, not to say divine, aspect:

> 'High on Olympus do the gods look down,
> On Isis, mother of the mighty Themmes,
> Her fruitful bankes, by Ceres and Pomona blest,
> Her silver Fludde, where pike and noble salmon rest...'

All very well as such stuff goes. Except that today the gods were in thwart mode. Before the sun was high enough to make the water blaze with light or turn the hedgerow shadows black, their engine changed its note – recovered for a few beats – coughed – then choked its way to silence. For several hundred yards the *Speedwell* resisted all efforts to steer her ashore, before the current took her, brushing in slow motion through a dense stand of purple loosestrife and into the towpath.

Whatever had ensnared the boat, there was no one but them to sort it. The river and its banks just went on looking like the deepest countryside, with no other creatures in sight except some cattle up to their hocks in the river, masticating a clump of rushes in the cause of a varied diet. Eliot got into his trunks, then into the dinghy; thence, all snorkelled up, into the water.

Only as he dived did he glimpse, beyond a thicket of sallow willows, some sign of human activity. Thick cables made a scrawl against the sky, and a generator hummed. He fancied he glimpsed at least one large mobile home. Squatters, was his thought; had to be, living in squalor on some dank meadow that lay flooded half the year.

Below its clear surface the river, slow-moving as mercury, was muddy and opaque. He worked his way by feel towards the propeller, over which lay a close-bonded sheath of weed. He had to remind himself that the engine, dammit, had definitely been disabled, even to tying up Monty, for whom switches and levers were only there to be leaped upon and pawed.

He surfaced, biffing his head against a suspended rubber fender, like a footballer trying a feeble header. As he reached into the dinghy for a pair of cutters he heard what sounded like someone shouting through a megaphone. Perhaps they'd blundered into some public scene of uproar, complete with protest banners and police dogs. Eliot dived again, and at his third descent the shaft and blades were free. All at the cost of nothing more than an inch-long gash on one knee, which he didn't notice till he stood on deck and Mike said, 'Shit!' Plus there was the sense that his thundering heart had expanded to make his head pulse like a harbour light.

If he'd been underwater long enough, he might also have thought himself hallucinating. Maybe not the second time he rose, when a great shadow fell across him, not from a police helicopter but a small dirigible grazing the treetops. But he was due at least a moment's self-doubt as he surfaced for a third time. He was sharing the river with three other creatures. A distant white horse with bouffant mane swam towards him. It bore two clean-limbed naked riders, a man and a long-haired girl. Distance had miniaturized them, to look like a teasing glimpse from Alice's Wonderland.

In the dirigible a camera whirred. A short way downstream, unheard by Eliot and his friends, a miked-up voice declared, '*Zuleika Dobson*, Scene 158, Take One...'

VII

Subject: Zuleika Dobson: A Turkey as Big as the Hindenburg.

Chris's career as a screenwriter had not ended well. It was doomed right from the promotion over him of That Female, a.k.a. raven-haired sodding Cressida Thingy. His departmental colleagues from the day job wouldn't have known him, had they seen the email intended to trumpet his resignation.

...And furthermore, just how is this movie supposed to be a comedy if it omits the book's thunderstorm scene, wherein the whole of Oxford University drowns itself for love of a silly woman?

... I won't demean either of us by saying this again. But just how do you propose substituting this mass-suicide sequence, as a climax, with a fearless crusading speech from Zuleika to the Duke and a hundred other undergraduates ('As you know, this is now the Edwardian age')? Whereupon they don't kill themselves, but pledge volunteer work at feminist-run orphanages in the

Himalayas?

... and if Zuleika is so all-seeing, and the Duke is 'like, a really, really clever guy, the smartest and funniest I've ever met, like he's part of my own DNA' plus he understands women after all, what in your opinion does motivate the action? ... In place of the gods looking down and laughing unkindly, may I shyly suggest, once again, that you can't hack it by inventing nothing more than two mortar-boarded frowsty codgers up Magdalen Tower, with a magic chessboard and a dastardly plan to thwart votes for women.

...and if your setting is still meant to be pre-World-War-I, do you seriously think our leads will have sex in a punt at first sight, then go post-coital shopping in some enormous Gothic-style mall resounding to multiple hurdy-gurdies?

...Perhaps my understanding is unequal to the vision that informs the script in its current form. But

(a) why exactly does Zuleika now thwart the Duke's death, by shinning up his best set of battlements with a sniper-scope and shooting the two black owls destined to predict his extinction, and

(b) why on earth should this sequence cut to both leads, naked, running together through a cornfield, then ditto riding a horse?

...Understand meanwhile that no one – how shall I put this? – is more concerned than I to give Cressida Venn, whom after all you personally approved as scriptwriter, every merest vestige of respect that may be her due ...

From a fourteen-page email, saved but never sent, by
Dr Chris Lovell, ex-screenwriter, to the board of Kraken
Productions Inc.

There was more film-making spoor outside the Cup and Ball inn, where they moored in quest for a late lunch. The car park was glutted; there were shiny metropolitan four-by-fours, a couple of people carriers, a tanker designed for several settings of film-shoot rain; and a 1928 Bugatti, polished enough to serve as a heliograph. Queueing at the bar Eliot recognized the delightful laugh, then the barnet, tousled but sleek, of a recent acquaintance: Cressida Someone, whom he must have met at work. By the time she turned and saw him, he remembered. His firm had arranged for her to have a free holiday with a group of clients walking the Hindu Kush, all found including carpeted goat-hair tents and an on-site chef whose repertoire included fresh-fruit jelly at twelve thousand feet. Of course, a journalist. To be fair, she'd given the business a stonking write-up.

Recognizing him, she was all astonishment and pleasure. She had violet eyes and the kind of pallor that goes with dazzling health. In the small corner of Eliot's soul that harboured any scepticism, he knew he was being zapped with so many measured units of purely professional welcome. Again, he supposed, fair enough. Introductions were made, which included the youngish, sun-tanned, uxorious-looking man who was with her.

'This, of course, is my husband. This is Jerry. My husband is here with the Kraken people. The studio has hired my husband as one of their script advisors.'

'Darling, you're the actual writer,' said Jerry, looking at his wife while shaking hands with Chris. As a spouse, he mixed self-abasement with triumphant ownership. Chris privately thanked the goddess of good luck for not letting him email his unbuttoned rant against this woman's contribution to world literature. He, and they, smiled and shook hands as if for a masterclass in schmooze.

Mike too was greeted as an old friend. For some reason he responded like a man who was expected to look dignified while being smacked on the nose. Eliot then remembered another connection: this was the person whom Mike, too full of righteous wrath to be original, mostly described as Jerry the Shit. The toe-rag and low fellow who'd deserted Bianca and the innocent children she'd only just borne him.

None of this disparagement had suggested itself to effluent Jerry, nor to his new wife; and when Cressida pressed Eliot and fellow crew members to join them outside, there was nothing to be done but show gratitude and say yes.

The place where they sat was a stone-paved terrace by a lawn. The pub seemed at first sight like many others, being covered in window-boxes and hanging baskets whose healthy petunias and begonias resembled a huge vegetable chest wig. In fact it had been built as the almshouse attached to a medieval priory. But unlike the nunnery at Foxcombe End, where Edith's clique of New Women had lived and quarrelled irreconcilably over their plans for utopia, little remained here to justify even a Department of the Environment plaque. The monks' great stone barn had survived, but mostly got ignored since it looked like hundreds of others in the Cotswolds. Over five centuries or so it had been a malt-house, a cavalry barracks, a local jail, and a bicycle repair shop; these days it was a garden centre.

A beautiful soaring church had left no trace, its ancient sculpted stones shipped downriver as rubble for various waterfront foundations. One hint of times past did remain, overlooking the pub garden. On the wall of the barn a row of early-Tudor arches were outlined, ghostly as human shadows burned into permanence by an atomic blast. They showed where work had just started on a cloister, then been forever stalled.

Before the abbey's almshouses were a pub, they'd become a farmhouse, its garden fertilized with ground-up bones from the smashed tombs of several holy priors. The inn's present name had been got from a large cup-shaped stone, once the base of a wayside cross; the 'ball' lying in it was all that remained of the cross's elegant Gothic pillar. With a new Leica that he'd almost believed was needful for this expedition, Eliot snapped away compulsively. At this stage of their holiday each bumpy meadow or broken limestone wall still taunted him with the chance that it might have been sketched by Aunt Edith or looted for some Georgian folly by 'Plenitude' Figg, their common ancestor. He'd started with the pub's best-known fitment, a human skull ornamented with silver to make a drinking cup. It occupied a glass case in the main bar and was described as being a fragment of the priory's founder who, legend said, would ceremonially wash his hands in the river each annual Maundy Thursday before giving money to the poor.

'Yeah, right,' Chris had said in disbelief, reading the caption that claimed to identify the skull. 'Seeing as it was discovered in a dunghill.'

There was a particular reason for the absence of ruins. After the monks got evicted and its land was privatised, much of their house of God had, as it were, been put through a matter transformer, coming out a couple of parishes downriver in the form of a Renaissance mansion. Eliot didn't care to say so, but Colnthrop Hall was another place that gave substance to his historical sense of identity. It too had figured in Aunt Edith's oeuvre, as part of a grand parkland scene including a memorial folly by Augustus Figg at his most classically overblown.

'I like the guys who could do that – just pull this place down and leave no trace,' said Mike. Politeness made him feel he should join in whatever people were talking about; unease in present company made him emphatic. 'They knew it took balls to follow the natural course of history, and outgrow the past. But they still went ahead and did it.' He frowned as he spoke, staring off at nothing and sitting even more than usually straight.

Chris avoided his eye and remarked, also for the sake of speaking, 'At least Horrible King Henry never declared a Year One. Whenever some idiot re-jigs the calendar, there's usually an increase in the body count.'

Cressida seemed scarcely to have heard them. She sat leaning against Jerry, face raised to the sun. 'This is our very own Year One, isn't it, darling?' From inside their invisible bubble of exclusivity he leaned and kissed her.

To Mike she said, 'I think you're so right. How can anyone respect themselves if they won't stand up for what they really want? Don't you agree, Jerry darling?'

'Sure. In private life as in the doings of state,' said Jerry, with an untroubled smile. 'You,' also looking at Mike, 'must understand that. By now, you probably know my ex-children better than I do. My two post-marital bastards.' His tone was cheerfully complicit; husband to husband in the fearless quest for personal fulfilment.

Cressida added, 'I'm sure they're terribly happy with you. After all, children are very resilient. I expect yours are the same – I mean, the children you had by, er, whoever you were married to before.'

It was surprising to see her blush; she clearly wasn't a woman who expected to falter, even in small things.

'*My* children,' said Mike, rigid with restraint, 'are both grown up.' He finished his pint, which he'd been sinking rather fast, and made an excuse to leave. With grim-visaged humour he muttered something about a flock of pregnant ewes nearby that the restive Monty needed to disrupt.

His friends watched him go, bearing himself like a man

who flinched from nothing, beyond personal dishonour.

Chris avoided everyone's eye until Mike had gone. Then he turned towards Cressida. 'So,' he asked disingenuously, 'How's the movie?'

'Zuleika?' Sudden delight seemed her response to most things. 'She's wonderful! I'm having such a great time making her relevant. A really vibrant character that contemporary audiences can relate to. Everyone's just getting ready to rehearse the sequence where she pilots a biplane. She's in a desperate race with the Duke, who's driving a stage coach with his family arms on it. We always knew this project would be such fun. Didn't we, darling?'

VIII

*What good people have in common is that they are
all different: each man blunders after salvation in
his own way. Only the wicked conduct themselves
by rote; that is why the sole distinction shared by
bad people is an absence of the unique.*

Attr. (some say) Oscar Wilde (1854-1900)

Next morning Mike was still missing a part of himself.
The power of decision, calm or at worst resolute, used to
be there in everything he did. Now it was absent, almost
as though a large muscle had been paralysed, something
dorsal or femoral, leaving only the need for a humbling
prosthesis.

Monty had had to be walked again, stopping every yard
or so to snuffle ecstatically at the muddy footpath. Drifts
of meadowsweet, heady-smelling, had to be fertilized
with a lopsided jet of canine piss; a lone fritillary, probably
the only one in the parish, got scraped away and its roots
crapped on; and groups of mallards, snoozing head under
wing on the riverbank, had to be disrupted into the
water by the pursuit of God knew what irresistible whiff.

Presumably a dog's nose, sensitive to every refinement of rankness or deliquescent bouquet, could turn its owner's life into a time-lapse movie. As in, so that's what swam or mated here, two days ago.

From the human point of view, Monty's life of leaping about for joy failed to compensate for one unignorable fact of dog-walking. It was tedious: eye-wateringly, knee-weakeningly, bowel-distendingly boring. At least poor old Monty had come as part of the marriage; so Mike could always brace up with the thought that getting a dog hadn't been his idea.

But given their rate of progress through the endless countryside, it irked him not to know how anyone had contrived that TV ad with a dog. The one where a Labrador pulls along a blonde on a skateboard at the full eight miles an hour, not stopping to crap on anything. They must have been selling something gynaecological, because the blonde's trousers were so tight and white. That, certainly, was the response of ... the person he'd been watching with – yes, come on: Anna, his whatever he should get on and start calling her now. She'd said ...

After breakfast he got into the dinghy and rowed downriver towards their next mooring, near Colnthrop Hall. Last night's dinner must be atoned for after an evening of extravagance at the Radcot Brill, signature dish brill with bitter orange sauce (or turbot if you were insane and had suffered a rush of blood to the wallet). Rigorous exercise was needed anyway this morning, to enliven the body and clear the mind. In Kosovo he'd known a chaplain from the Berkshires who'd confided that he could only really pray when jogging or working out. Mike was a dogmatically godless man; but he'd understood what the padre meant. It was easier to think when he was striving down the river, doing his stint of so many strokes per day.

Everything, he was convinced, would come good, be fine, whatever, once he and Bianca could properly begin their life together. When this holiday was over, they should make a serious effort to decide how and where they wanted to live, long term. The houseboat had stood for the very principle they cherished – of travelling light, and being together as free spirits. It still did – of course it did. But there lurked the fact – since when, he wouldn't care to say – that some people saw it otherwise.

Actually he did recall the first dissenting voice – though it should be said it only came from Bianca's mother. She'd come over on a visit a couple of months ago. Her arrival had been preceded by a series of emails, mostly in Portuguese but switching to accurate if unfluent English whenever Mike was personally addressed. They'd made it clear that Signora Pereira intended her forthcoming trip as a lap of honour, from which she could survey Bianca's newly restored prosperity.

'We all know you are the man to lift up our only daughter in this world, back to the place where all of us deserve to see her.'

At the time, he hadn't been sure how to understand this. Enlightenment first kicked in outside Gatwick Terminal South.

'Is this your car?' he was asked, as he arrived, complete with twins in their baby-seats, and got out to help with the luggage. A question like that, whether or not it was levelled at Mike's dirty but inoffensive Volvo, could have had one of many meanings – if other sharp-eyed queries hadn't followed.

On seeing the houseboat his new mother-in-law had asked him, 'Is this where you bring the children at weekends?' With entitled directness she'd added, 'I thought you had a big yacht.'

The proportion of English spoken had fallen thereafter. Mike's command of Portuguese was not quite up to guidebook standard, despite evening classes plus an attempted regime of tutorials from Bianca – which she approached with less determination than he would have hoped.

'Oh, I know you'll learn all these things anyway.'

The two women were now apt to talk mostly to each other, like aristocrats too grand to practise discretion in front of the servants, with Mike understanding maybe one sentence in three. But it was clear enough that his mother-in-law had shed the air of rejoicing she'd advertised at their wedding. It was also evident that, though the day was warm, the tide was at the full, and the sun struck brilliance from the calm, busy river, lunch on the little deck aft of the houseboat just wouldn't do. Instead they managed to transport themselves, children, favoured stuffed toys, bulging nappy bag, dog and mother-in-law, to a nearby pub that had a garden – indispensable if either infant started shrieking at any length – but which didn't do high chairs, so that he and Bianca each sat with a twin on their lap, coaxing them to eat their nice ravioli.

At least it gave him somewhere to look, dodging the occasional biff in the face from little Claudia's plastic spoon, once the conversation seemed to intensify. The reason wasn't hard to guess, as significant looks were cast up at the nearby waterfront block where, um, Anna had recently moved in.

His mother-in-law, sitting on the other side of her daughter, leaned forward to catch his eye.

'Some people,' she said, 'have no business to take your money from you.' She glowered upwards, then back at him, to indicate the tenth floor of the new apartment building, with its glass-fronted balconies and general look of banal shiny comfort. 'Nor,' she added, 'to take from you your home. The house that should now be the home of your wife and her little children.'

There followed an exchange in Portuguese in which Bianca was told much the same, plus the fact that a real man would know how to defend his own against usurpers.

'That apartment is nothing to do with me,' he said, more sharply than one should, he realized, when holding a small child. 'My wife – my ex-wife – my ex-wife and the mother of my children' – why he put that in, God knows – 'bought it with her share of the money we'd agreed to divide between us.'

For the first time in their marriage, he'd been angry. Not with Bianca, thank God – not with his wife. Never, he assured himself, could he be cross with her.

In fact, now he'd seen his mother-in-law being insolent rather than embarrassing, he was convinced he adored his wife even more. There'd been nothing – certainly nothing he could follow – in the exchanges with her mother to suggest that Bianca tolerated Signora Pereira's shabby opinion of him. Throughout all the older woman's seemingly pointed utterances at his expense, did his wife do anything more than bow her head, avoid his eye and stay mute. And in all the broad landscape of their shared life to come, it was impossible that Bianca would ever join her mother in describing, uh, his ex, as 'that woman'.

Rowing hard down the quiet Isis, he now found his solitude disrupted by a thought so unwelcome that he almost slowed and drifted to a stop. As Bianca's erstwhile, Jerry the Shit embodied everything in marriage that Mike prided himself on not being. But just once, he'd had a point.

Only the one, of course.

On first hearing of Shitty Jerry's delinquencies, starting with his transfer of affection from Bianca to the scarcely nameable Cressida, Mike's indignation had burst forth and spread itself over everything the man had said or done. Almost the worst offence was disrespect to Bianca's family.

'He called my mother an awful thing –'

'Good God! He called her that?'

'No – no. That's not what he said. An awful word – that's what he said. A terrible word. Only, I'm not sure what it is, in English.'

At length, via question and answer, and a dictionary, they'd translated the deplorable word – 'this horrid big smelly creature, that I know never existed.'

'A *behemoth?!*'

... Recalling the incident, Mike heard himself bark with laughter, as violently as if a small demon had been expelled. Immediately he felt the dank breath of guilt at his own disloyalty. Bending his back to the oars, he rowed on.

I X

Reader! Pass not by without a tear
Since that Earth's finest Hound lies here...

From an anonymous poem on the tomb of Primussimus, a
wolfhound, Colnthrop Hall, Oxfordshire, 1738

'I'm thinking of having something like this put up for
Monty, when he goes,' Mike said.

In life, Primussimus can't have done badly. In death
he outclassed his noble owner plus most other persons of
quality within twenty miles. From the *Speedwell*'s mooring
a lane, then a parkland path, led towards his memorial,
fifteen feet high atop a low hill that bore his name. A
steep-sided pyramid featured a sculpted cartouche with
symbols of the chase. At its summit sat a life-size statue
of the august woofer himself; and on its squared-off base
eight elegantly graven verses declared his virtues as Loyal
Companion and Truest Friend.

From Primussimus' Tump, with its view of four
counties, Eliot led his crew smartly on, with a mutter of,
'Not quite my period.' Augustus 'Plenitude' Figg probably
would have snaffled this commission too, but only if he'd

lived twenty years sooner. The place Eliot said they sought was at the furthest corner of the park, near the head of a shallow combe. In Aunt Edith's painting of it, the oak woods planted to close off the view were purplish and brushed with winter sun, and curved along the skyline like a somnolent brute. Her *Streams Meeting: the Confluence of the Rivers Wyndall and Fleme* scarcely hinted at the elaborate grotto fashioned by Eliot and Edith's common ancestor, against whose darkness stood a fountain plus a couple of stone naiads romping nicely together in its waters as personifications of the two little rivers.

The model for one nymph was unidentified; presumably a local girl. But the other was fairly well known to art history, as L'Écossaise, an innkeeper's daughter from Stirling. When she was seventeen a passing English lordling, with extensive grouse moors the least part of his recent inheritance, was so smitten that he took her with him to Paris, where he died of consumption, being en route for Rome and a better climate. History glimpses her causing a sensation there in a sumptuous establishment known as the Temple of the Muses. Her interpretation of Epicuria, so-called, featured her being brought to table on a vast silver dish, wearing nothing but a delicate pink sauce. She was painted several times by Boucher, and is best known for his bewitching nude portrait of her as *Mary Magdalene Repentant*, now in the Louvre, where a token skull finds itself in a face-off against her own finest assets.

Other people were making a pilgrimage here to see her image. German was being spoken, to a group of onlookers in comfortable shoes chosen with as much seriousness as the expedition itself had been. From their scuffed and faded chic and the close attention they paid their guide, these were the sophisticated, well-off sort of people on whom Eliot's business had thrived. They were looking around, rather knowledgeably, at the half-reconstructed grotto, which was currently roofed with a naked wooden framework resembling a mass of skeletal stalagmites.

Eavesdropping, Chris half-thought he heard his name spoken elsewhere, from behind him. By the rim of the fountain, less purposeful than the Germans but closed up tight as herded sheep, there stood a smaller group. Old or young, they were better dressed, but bore a look of dispossession nonetheless. Chris heard someone say his name again, and recognized his cousin Imogen. Bussed out from Todington Hall no doubt, on one of the day trips offered by that top-of-the-heap mental asylum/residential home/whatever the hell one was supposed to call her present gaff. No wonder the socially excluded trustafarians alongside her wore so much expensive branding. Imogen's late father had put her somewhere so pricey you almost expected a charge for clean air.

But it was cheering to see her like this, in the sunlit out-of-doors at a public place. Chris couldn't remember when she'd last been allowed something so hopeful and convalescent. She even smiled and spread her arms in greeting. It didn't make her into a grown-up. But it was still a shock to glimpse her former self. Fifteen maybe, and still childlike enough to be thrilled at everything life offered.

'Hello, Chris! Hello, Mike! Hello, Eliot! Hello! Hello!'

Not unaffectedly cheerful. More likely under the influence of uppers, and trying to compensate for years of accumulated shyness. But still.

Chris hugged her. He and Martha were always careful to do so, whether or not Imogen seemed to know who they were. She was wearing jeans and an ill-judged T-shirt, a so-called classic printed with a photo of Marilyn Monroe. He'd been there when her mother, of all people, had given it as a birthday present. As if she were blind to the contrast between Imogen's wan face versus the image of Marilyn, head back, eyes half closed, appearing to breathe out as though her leftover carbon dioxide was everyone else's elixir of life.

Certainly that's what Chris had told Aunt Leonora.

'Darling,' she'd said with regal certainty, 'that girl needs things she can measure up to.'

Chris had backed off. He owed this woman so much, he had to believe she meant everything for the best.

Today it said something for Imogen's enlivened state that Marilyn showed her up scarcely at all. She was still round-shouldered, from years of being hunched into her unhappy private self. But maybe that was just habit.

She murmured, 'I don't think their guide' – indicating the postgraduate student in charge of the Germans – 'is telling them everything he ought to.' She pointed at the Scots lass, sculpted in dignified abandon and representing the Wyndall Brook. 'That one's called Vindelia. And the other one's Flumentilla. And it's not really Wyndall, it's Widdle. And their silly Roman names are just made up.

They were invented when those statues were done.' She gestured, enlivened by certainty. 'Back in the days of the naming of the rivers,' she exclaimed, 'when the Old English ruled this land, that's not what they were called. *She* was Bigga! And *she* was Flucc!'

One or two of the Germans looked round. Eliot twitched with pedantry, as always at someone who mightn't know who came first, Pocahontas or Sir Lancelot. He was silenced by a glance from Chris.

'*And* they were protectresses of nature, all along their own river. *Her* special plant is the lady's smock, and *hers* is the willow tree, which is why when they walk among us as fairies that one wears a mauve tunic, and *she* has pale green wings like a dragon-fly's.'

Chris said nothing, recognizing two book plates from the *Flower Fairies* series he'd given Imogen for her seventh birthday. Hoping to be tactful, Mike asked, 'How do you know this?'

'I dreamed it. And that's how I know that this place is the hub of an Earthstar. There are ley lines from here. Lines of power. One goes to Silbury Hill, one goes to Maiden Castle, one goes to the well at Glastonbury Abbey.'

'Not the Tor?'

'No, Mike, not Glastonbury Tor; that's a silly idea. And not everybody appreciates this. But from every one of those places, that means there's a straight line. Right through to here. To where the goddesses' streams meet.'

All three of them were rescued from looking embarrassed or impatient by the fact that Imogen's party were leaving. Seeing her fellow patients about to be moved on, like an under-rehearsed chorus in a school play, she lingered, putting a hand through Chris's arm.

'Can I come and see you all? Can I? I know Mummy will say I can, if you ask her.' Her look, usually vacant or veiled, was fever-bright. Give marks for endeavour, thought Chris. His twenty years of university teaching had familiarized him with most things people her age did to fake self-confidence.

'And I'll cook for you. You said you were taking it in turns to cook. I can fix lunch.'

'Uh, I didn't know you could cook.' He tried to picture Imogen and the other inmates as masters of seething-pans and flaming hobs. Knives fit to razor off the head of a three-quarter-ton ox. Medicated or not, most of them looked bland and harmless enough to cease existence where they stood, like movie characters at the hand of some CGI pixelmeister.

'I can cook better than lots of people. I've read all sorts of books about it. About vegetarian cooking. I know all kinds of stuff about plants of virtue. And plants of prophecy...Please ask Mummy if I can.'

'Of course I will.' Chris knew better than to hesitate, and betray unease. Even on drugs, Imogen had moments of insight that made her quick as any all-powerful psychiatric grandee.

He added as they parted, 'I'll do it right away.' Always take on the most challenging job first. Sure enough, as they strolled back towards Primussimus' monument, he was through to his aunt's private line.

'...No, it's fine, Leonora,' he sort-of lied. 'If that's what will spread happiness, I'm ready to take responsibility.' In fact he found the new, energised Imogen mysterious and dauntingly unpredictable.

'In that case, Crispin darling' – his aunt's one foster-maternal failing, in his eyes, was that she always called him by his detested full name – 'it will do her good. I'm glad this is on her own initiative for once. Now, you'll need her new address … yes, I'm having her moved in a couple of days, though I'm sure she can still be seen by the same sort of people often enough, on the NHS.'

There followed multiple directions as to times, place and procedures. Meanwhile, above the view from Primussimus' grassy Tump, by unspoken consent they all slowed down and paused.

Eliot's phone sounded.

'Marina! … Er …Hi.'

'Eliot. I'm more sorry for this than I can say.'

'Uh …?'

'I know I shouldn't be taking up your time. Not when you're on holiday. I'm sure every moment is precious to you, if not in the same way as when you're at work, and I feel even worse that I'm the one contacting you like this, because I, more than anyone out of all the world, am the person most likely to understand just how much you don't want to be disturbed…'

Eliot's look of forgiveness was in place before he knew it. 'That's fine… no, really…' He even found himself nodding, as if importunate Marina could zap him long-range with an all-seeing, gloopily mascara'd eye.

With the others taken up, it occurred to Mike that he

was late with his daily call to Lisbon.

'Darling ...'

'Darling ...'

The two babies were fine, all the aunts and cousins were fine, the neighbours were good too, and he didn't forget to ask about her grandmother and her mother. He even remembered not to say that he'd met the father of her children, with his new wife.

'So ...'

'So ... you're on a big boat, with your friends ...'

'Well, yes, it's a splendid big boat.' A pause threatened, and he struggled to recall some details. 'It's so extravagant and luxurious, it has the latest design of echo-sounder. And radar technology.'

'That does sound very extravagant and luxurious. I shall tell my mother about them.'

'Yes. Eliot is very proud of his boat.'

If they sounded like a Linguaphone record, it must be because they weren't used to being apart. Until now there could have been few conversations when they weren't in one another's arms.

She said, 'I shall think of you, with your echo-sounder and radar. Just you and your two friends alone on that big boat.'

'That's right ...'

'There are just three of you, aren't there?'

'Well, yes -'

'So you haven't met any pretty ladies on the way?'

'Well, no -'

'Haven't you met anyone?'

Dutifully Mike described their pilgrimage to the scene of Edith's *Streams Meeting*, and the encounter with Imogen.

'Is she a pretty lady?'

'Well, I suppose she could be -'

'You must know if your friend's cousin is pretty. You must surely know this, if she is, when you have all of you just met her, and, I have no doubt, told each other what you think of her ...'

On the lifelong journey he'd elected to share with Bianca, a small change of vista was threatening to edge into view.

'...And is she going to visit you, on the boat where all of you are living? ...'

For the sake of privacy they'd fanned out, and stood, three men in a bait, each facing away from Primussimus' majestic doggy image. Were he alive, the great wolfhound's gaze declared, he still wouldn't have stooped to notice them, neither humans nor plebeian hound. Especially not Monty, who'd just lifted a leg to release an hydraulic-strength jet of piss on the verse describing Primussimus in the stonemason's finest Augustan script as an Apotheosis of the canine Kind.

On the line to Eliot, at last Marina was tacking towards her reason for calling.

' ... I know you did speak to Roly, a short while ago. And he did say – I hope it's all right for me to repeat this – I mean, what I do know is that he really enjoyed meeting you.'

'I thought he was very easy to talk to.' These days,

when Eliot had anything to do with Marina, he couldn't help sounding, well, kindly. Nothing was left of his former self, a boy divorcee struggling to divide his days and nights between part-time jobs and evening class. Marina's subsequent marriages had each met with shipwreck, then dissolved in a sea of flotsam and regret. His younger self could almost believe the two of them had invented sex; by now that boy might never have existed.

'I'm so glad you got on. Do you know, that's what everyone has always said about Roly, even when he was little.'

Except his father. Marina's most recent husband had been a diplomat, whose world of embassy life and its correctitudes had brought out the utmost in her. No one was more determined to confuse a successful life of her own with sitting on various Diplomatic Wives' committees, whose members ruthlessly queue-jumped in the Ladies Powder Room according to their spouse's rank. Marina spared nothing and no one in striving to put her husband the third attaché and his prospects at the centre of her life. Divorce, though, had brought no bonuses for trying. Marina's latest ex had resolutely cut himself off, not only from her, but from their son, whom he'd ever since described as some kind of by-blow.

It was hard to know if Roland really needed help. Eliot doubted Marina was just chasing this job as a proud parent who thought nothing too good for her boy. More likely what drove her was the illusion that here, at least, she could exercise patronage. To Marina, achieving something her son couldn't do for himself would be a prize without equal. To be the one bringing him the job he wanted, she'd make even pride like hers into a blood sacrifice.

Wary of making false promises, he said, 'We weren't able to talk for long.'

'Oh, but Roly said you'd really covered quite a lot of ground, in the time.'

'And there are several things that still need straightening out. Before I decide what to do with the company.'

'Of course. I mean, starting when you get back from the holiday, I suppose.'

Cautiously he agreed, 'I did say I'd be in touch with Roland after that.'

'When you're in London, yes ...'

'Yes ...'

'Yes... I'm sorry. I know you did say that. You said that, I know. I'm sorry. Eliot, I'm sorry. Goodbye ...'

X

The wild being better than the tame, [Parsnip is good for] the Bitings of Serpents ...[Dill] is a gallant expeller of wind...

Nicholas Culpeper (1616-1654)

Sith Garlicke then hath power to save from death, Beare with it though it makes unsavoury breath; And scorne not Garlicke, like to some that think It onely makes men winke, and drinke, and stinke...

Sir John Harington (1561-1612)

Between turns at the wheel Chris was sprawled on deck in a canvas chair and frowning at images of, among others, his younger self. On a sun-splattered screen he held a recording of Leonora's latest TV appearance, this time in a documentary detailing her life both at work and as a wife and mother. He'd have found this easier to view down in his cabin with the curtains drawn and all the calm, bright vistas of willows and meadowland banished; but blow that.

'Darling, I expect you were too busy to catch the broadcast, weren't you?' his aunt said when he'd called after meeting Imogen in Colnthrop Park.

Guiltily he'd recalled that every frame was still unviewed.

'It's on my iPad, to help with my speech about Uncle Hugh,' he'd replied, and was grateful when she left it at that. Chris avoided telling untruths, for the reason that he was no good at it. 'Dad, you're a rubbish liar,' Tom would say. 'And that's no reason you should be pleased with yourself. Always telling the truth isn't a virtue, it's just a socio-economic handicap.' Tom usually delivered such flourishes with a grin, as affection jostled against relentless showing off.

Chris tried to concentrate on the documentary. Impossible now, to view this piece of old film without a sense of reality slipping a cog. He remembered it being shot, by one of the many staff who eased the workings of Aunt Leonora's domestic life and enabled her career. On the sunlit lawn of their weekend home, there they were in a smiling family group. Leonora's column as an agony aunt had featured her own household a lot. At first they'd figured against a background of small accidents and happy chat; later, with Imogen as something more poignant than just a troubled teen, Aunt Leonora's tone had changed to one of valiant frankness…

But was there anything here to inspire his memorial speech? Chris had lost count of his discarded first lines.

'It may be that any one of you gathered here today might have spoken of my uncle more fittingly …'

'To begin with the one inescapable fact: I owe him so much ...'

'Some of you may have heard how generous Hugh's other bequests must also have been. I only know that as his nephew ...'

In vain he squinted at the screen. Here was film of Imogen, maybe three years old, and bright as a new-made daisy chain. The rest of them – teenage Chris and Leonora herself – looked cheerful enough. Uncle Hugh, inevitably, was the one guying at the camera.

The programme cut to Leonora as she looked now: sitting on a lakeside lawn overhung by great trees. Shading her from the sun was an elegant little canvas pavilion with a conical roof and flaps hooked back like theatre curtains. Her chair stood to one side of a garden table, as if space had been made for one other person. Sure enough, the film dissolved backwards through ten years or so, to when the other chair held Uncle Hugh, so that the two of them sat, each reading a book, like the conjoined halves of a diptych. Thence back to the present and Leonora alone by her husband's empty seat. For a few seconds she was held in shot, elegiacally framed from the middle distance.

Chris froze the film and put the iPad aside, only to score out another failed first line.

'How hard it is, standing before you all, to show respect by reducing a life – and such a life – to nothing more than ...'

One thing making his task so massive was that Hugh's bequest wasn't just figures on a printout. Nor was it merely a valuable object you could put away in a safe. Its image looked up at him now, paused on his iPad.

'Yes,' Imogen had said. 'Daddy's given you that house.' As so often on the phone, her voice held no shade of meaning he could detect; you'd never think she was describing the family home, where all their early histories blended. It was a beautiful building, too; mostly plate glass and baulks of oak, the architect's most celebrated yet. Uncle Hugh had been rich: possessed of booty in the order of hog-swilling and platinum-plated. No case there for fannying about with descriptions like 'comfortable', 'well off' or 'not doing too badly at all'. Yet with his uncle looking set to live another twenty years, it hadn't occurred to Chris to wonder if he himself might one day inherit something. Now, just thinking of such a bequest made him euphoric, in the way he imagined taking some class A pharmaceutical. The sort where a second sniff might turn the whole world into the feel-good movie of your life.

His cousin had added, 'It's only a resort house. That's what Mummy says.' Again she'd spoken without feeling, like a small child parroting its elders. And how like poor Imogen to quote anyone so that their real meaning was confounded. ('I'm thrilled for you, darling,' his aunt had said, after the will was read.)

*

Neither Chris's speech nor the *Speedwell* had got much further thirty-six hours on, as they waited at their mooring by the Dog and Decoy for the taxi bringing Imogen from … however one described her new address.

'It's a residential home,' Leonora had said. 'And I'm assured that of its kind it's very good. Maybe there she'll learn to stand on her own two feet. Even now, the least she could do would be to help organise her own party.' The *Speedwell*'s one unbreakable engagement, so Chris considered, was a dinner to be given on a boat a few days downriver, for Imogen's birthday.

And here was his cousin, getting out of a people-carrier hired just for her by one of her mother's secretarial staff. Pre-paid of course, so that Imogen needn't be confused by having to handle money.

'They changed my meds!' she exclaimed, bounding towards him and delivering a hug. Embracing him on her own initiative, just like that. At least she didn't seem to be on downers. And – he hadn't noticed this before – wasn't she looking like someone who could be pretty? The way she had been, some years back?

As if hearing his thought, she added, 'Maybe soon I can show everyone a change of me!'

On board, she surveyed their galley with a look of purpose.

'Now – !'

'How do you like Eliot's boat?' said Chris. Whereas Mike was already shaved, breakfasted and rowing his allotted distance downstream, Eliot, all stubble and pyjamas, was moving with a convalescent's care as he tried introducing his hangover to strong coffee and buttered toast. Not that he wouldn't still care what anyone thought about the *Speedwell*, despite last night's after-effects.

'Oh, yes!' said Imogen. 'We used to have one just like

this – do you remember, Chris? Now – I've got a menu all written down. Please may I look in your cupboards? I want to see if you've got what I need. Of course this is your lunch, Chris – I know it's your turn to cook. But I shall help you. I think you should have a vegetarian theme for today. Now, I've ruled out the broad-bean pate and the celeriac remoulade – see, even though they're written down, here – because we don't want to make things difficult for ourselves. Besides, the spirits of the dead reside in every kind of *Leguminosa*, including *Vicia faba*.'

'Uh?' said Eliot, musty-eyed as hell, but still hoping to look polite.

'Broad beans, of course. And I don't think we'll bother with parsley, either. Everybody knows it grows better for a wicked person than for a good one. But I don't mind including potatoes if you don't. Some people won't use them, because they're not in the Bible. But I think that's just superstitious ...Oh. You haven't got potatoes anyway. Really, all you have got is this breakfast stuff. And all this, er, Calvados and vodka and things. But we can probably manage with what you have got. Only you'll want to lend me some scissors. And, Chris, I need you to help me come out and forage. Have you got a penknife and a small trowel ... Oh, one of these serving spoons will do for digging ...

'Now, here's the menu I've brought; of course it's only a work in progress, as anyone can see. What we end up having for lunch will depend on what we find growing by the river... Look, I've written down a green salad – that'll be easy; we'll find lots of things like ground elder and hairy bittercress in the hedgerow bottoms round here. And I've written down dock pudding, and nettle haggis, and maybe we can think about a wheat casserole. And if we find watercress, that'll be useful to make green eggs. Everyone knows you can easily kill off the liver-fluke larvae if you just boil it long enough. Oh – and fat-hen leaves are bound to be good, because they were part of the ceremonial last meal fed to that strangled man in Denmark who they found a thousand years afterwards in a bog.'

'Well,' said Chris, with every appearance of cheerfulness, 'so long as he wasn't made to eat up as a penance for something.' He'd once been obliged to take part in a similar exhumation and dissection, at a Viking site in southern Greenland. Maybe lunch could be postponed, to where it became an early supper. Preceded by going to the pub in quest for an alcoholic hunger so heroic, they'd be ready to masticate the cookbook itself.

Throughout the next hour, Monty was in snuffling and tail-wagging heaven. Not only were the two humans who walked him disinclined to hurry; they even helped with some of the digging. Each south-facing hedgerow had to be examined by them, while he himself sought out every gamey or foetid pungency with a thoroughness he hadn't been permitted since ending his career as an agent of the law. Only Imogen could have been as busy, as she truffled and snipped and rabbited on.

Chris meanwhile found himself passive as a husband left to wait outside a ladies' fitting room. His job was to loiter at Imogen's side and hold open a reinforced plastic carrier for her to fill, while making benign feedback noises.

'…Really? I never knew that about crow-flowers. Or furmitory …'

'Oh, yes. We've got to leave those alone. And we don't want ladies' mantle, either. It's an astrological plant of Venus. We don't want her. Or anything else that heats the blood. But if we can find marsh mallow roots, they're very useful against all sorts of things. Like excoriation of the guts. And the King's Evil…Let's have this mint. It's ever so powerful against nervous crudities. And I want to find some *Angelica sylvestris*, because it's the flower of the Archangel St Michael, who cast out the devil…'

Back at length on board, what fungal and vegetable treasures poured forth from the giant shopping bag. What dicing of wild fennel and what garlicky oozings pressed out from the root of the ramson, found in a white drift under some hawthorn trees. And what decapitation of dandelions and rubber-gloved stripping of stinging nettles, along with such casting of looks, hopeful or wary, at what had to be at least a kilo of horse mushrooms, gritty with the dried-out cow poo that had brought them to such a size. What swatches of comfrey, of yarrow and Jack-by-the-hedge.

'That smells good,' said Mike, coming aboard into a smoke-and-steam-filled galley. Having been down the river all this time, he was no better informed than he might be about the likely realities of lunch. And at this stage the odour of mushrooms fried with wild garlic was every bit as hopeful as the now-start-drooling boom of a dinner gong heard after hours of fasting. He was actually too late for some courses, but he made up for it by tucking in as readily as any other man who'd just rowed six miles.

For Eliot and Chris, delighted disillusionment set in as soon as they'd sat down and gingerly picked up their gobbling irons. Against all rational expectation, the tastes were even better than the smell. The mushrooms garnished a paella whose subtleties conspired to tease the palate before touching down on the pyloric sphincter amidst a quiet satisfaction that reigned throughout the meal. A green salad was served, in a wide ceramic bowl of a hand-painted design that looked fit to eat in its own right. The flavours, in a light oil-and-lemon dressing, were symphonic: fresh and aromatic, succulent and tangy, spicy and mild. Chris tried in vain to remember the salad's many ingredients, which had seemed at the time so repulsive; did they really include chickweed and good King Henry? The wild-fennel soup was a benign revelation; so too the elderflower fritters, crispy yet with a perfumed after-taste.

'And now,' said Imogen, serious as ever, though blushing faintly at their congratulations, 'Chris has said he'd cook the next course.'

True, he had. At the time it had seemed unfair as well as risky, to leave doing everything to his cousin. But it troubled him, now he was reminded. Cooking usually held neither fear nor puzzlement for Chris. But here, on the boat, location was all; and even the *Speedwell*'s array of electronics, from the waffle iron upwards, didn't counter the fact that at the only village shop within five miles it had been early closing. There were pubs along this part of the river, but only where someone had built an ancient bridge. Otherwise the *Speedwell* floated, lonely as a claustrophobic, laundry-strung spacecraft, through a green desert inhabited only by Friesians half up to their udders in damp grass. And even the crew's huge-seeming initial shop, back in Lechlade, had only extended to hangover cures and cooked breakfasts.

'I'll see what I can do. It may be the sort of thing that only looks good on the printed page.'

At the hob, Chris acted with a decisiveness that would have outdone Mike himself under shellfire. Before anyone could sense his apprehensions, he'd shovelled the just-cooked contents of the big frying pan onto four plates, then stepped back with a cry of, 'This should be the test of anyone's ability to say the right thing.'

Mike said, 'Can't you pitch this stuff better than that. Whatever it is. You always were crap at presentation.'

Eliot looked at what was on his plate. 'It's lucky,' he ventured, 'that we had some eggs.'

They ate carefully, as if checking each mouthful for razor blades. Eliot managed to sound almost neutral as he said, 'It's got Calvados in it!'

'I know that's not what one expects, in an omelette. Even when there's no milk or butter left.'

Mike, more forthright, remarked, 'It's certainly interesting. And unusual.'

A few moments on, Chris admitted, 'I have to say, I am desolated. *Je suis désolé.* Let no man nor woman feel they have to integrate their person with any more of this.'

Monty was the only dissenter, pleased and grateful no matter how gross the portion he was served. His appetite and his doggy goodwill both held up, an example to all, long after lunch was placed before him on the floor in restaurant French, as *oeufs extrêmes*: the eggs of extremity.

X I

Parvillaflora non-mangere. A humble plant of hedge and wayside: winged stems, small pinnate leaves, tiny white star-shaped flowers with stipules. Commonly known as greater lousewort; other names include white tare-fitch, stoat-snout, and Nick-get-out-of-bed.

Traditionally notorious as an hallucinogen, a piece of foliage equal to a square centimetre being enough to recast everyday reality as something else, though often without arousing suspicion in the victim. No change of mood is associated with this drug, though Culpeper (1649) admits that 'it doth wondrously provoke the Swimmings of the Braine even as it heateth not the Blood'.

In more recent times it has made an occasional appearance in crime fiction. During the so-called golden age of whodunits Agatha Christie, herself a former chemistry researcher, made use of its delayed effect — up to two days — in order to befuddle a key witness, as in her 1932 novel, *The Mystery of the Boathouse Murders*...

From an unidentified on-line source

However happily they'd scoffed the best parts of lunch on board, one ingredient had gone unnoticed. Plucked by accident from a hedge bottom along with a fistful of meadowsweet leaves, a couple of fragments from a plant of *P. non-mangere*, by no means both the same size, were now voyaging unsuspected through the digestive tract of two crew members.

Meanwhile they came to Oxford town. Within sight of it, anyway: a skyline of trees and spires beyond the sun-and-shadow-swept plain of Port Meadow. Yesterday, after the same half-ton people carrier had returned Imogen to her highly regarded residential home, they'd cast off and driven onward beneath a vast sunset feathered with mare's-tail cloud. The weather was set fine for days to come, and radio forecasts spoke of drought; it was an evening for puttering downriver until the light was almost gone. Eventually the *Speedwell* moored beneath a row of black poplars majestically leaning in unison, whose trunks gleamed luminescent to westward while their east side stood night-time dark.

Breakfast was eaten downriver from the bridge at Godstow, the place of God. Eliot had insisted on rising early again, pacing about at sunrise through what was left of the medieval nunnery, where aunt Edith had once sketched a tree and a fragment of wall. He'd woken on the *Speedwell*'s roof at daybreak in a dew-sodden sleeping bag, having guessed that most of the ruins were so crumbled away to pasture, they could only be made out in an early raking light. After scurrying back and forth with his camera, he'd got into his bunk and slept for another four hours.

Each of them was going into Oxford with his own private agenda. Eliot planned to drive the boat to a mooring in the city centre, at the Ferret and Fishcake pub near the river's junction with the Oxford Canal where it came down from the Cherwell valley and the Midlands. He was on his way to look at an interior painted by Edith depicting one of the grandest College chapels. At least, that's what the picture was supposed to show. She'd certainly made a stonking job of the light smiting its way through the huge east window; the interior itself was vague, like the inside of a spaceship gone too close to the sun.

He'd checked the college's public opening times, by phone as well as on line; but he'd still felt the need for a personal appointment to view. Even though his friends wouldn't be there to see, what counted most for Eliot in such a place was not being humbled as a seeming trespasser: '*Are* you a member of this College, sir?'

After breakfast Chris unlashed his bike from the roof of the boat, in anticipation of a lunch date with his former tutor.

'Just paying a visit to Professor Aylwin.'

Mike said, 'I thought you'd always been on first-name terms.'

'Yes, but that sounds pretentious now he's an uberdude.' When Chris had first known him, the good Professor had been plain Doctor, young, overworked and scarcely able to pay the mortgage on a four-room terraced home near the canal; now he was the College President. Chris was also playing down the reality of lunch. Not a snack in a pub garden, but a gathering in college where he was the principal guest.

'Bugger how the food tastes,' Eliot had once said, on hearing Chris was off to a college gaudy.

'Not bad, actually –'

' – I mean the inedible stuffed swan or whatever. But where else do you get the presentation?'

Eliot's idea of himself as an academic outsider was innocent of any crabbiness or cynicism. Rather, it fed his uncritical pleasure in antique rituals: the Senior Scholar standing up to read the Latin grace; the wearing of gowns in Hall. Plus someone involved with the meal, maybe the college chef, maybe a visiting philologist, who knew you didn't just carve a dish: bream should be described as splayed, plovers were mined and mallards, unbraced. Eliot relished leftover tradition whether or not it connected to his own past. The scholar in him had an unshakeable grasp of abstract political ideas and the onward march of impersonal social forces. Yet history, to him, was still nothing if not dates and places, much as some people's sense of self evaporates without a home full of holiday souvenirs and framed snapshots.

Mike was evasive about his own reasons for going into town. From the way he'd muttered, 'A few errands; I won't be long,' you'd expect him to sidle or slouch as he set off; instead he strode out at four-and-a-half miles an hour, straight-backed as Monty himself in human form.

The others suspected where he was going. But until he was out of earshot they said nothing.

Alone, Eliot drove his treasured boat into Oxford,

for him as others a city of dreams and desires. At his side, upright on a matching chair, Monty sat, alert as any ceremonial consort, his ears flowing in the breeze. The boat was moored outside their rendezvous, Monty was tied up to stand guard, and Eliot set off, fulfilled as any athlete who hears the starting gun for a race he's bound to win.

Yes, well, then Marina rang again ... Still, no day can be perfect ...

She had little to say that was new, starting with how she hated being a nag. Eliot was usually the personification of good faith; but today he found himself taking refuge in small pale-grey lies.

'I may not know what new appointments to make, until we get to London. Since some of the business may still be at risk...'

'Oh, surely not!' Marina was neither selfish nor hard hearted. But womanly reassurance, coming from her, always sounded wrong, like she'd studied how in a manual.

She added, 'You're being very generous, all the same. After, you know, what I did.'

Eliot had to think before he remembered what she meant. Leaving him for a better bet was what. Five years older, a guy with his own sports car, plus the Marina-rated heaven of a small trust fund. The boy-man Eliot had stormed, and she had apologized and wept; but she'd insisted on going. Much later he'd barely credit his relief at how things had turned out.

But he knew she preferred to be resented rather than pitied. Gallantly he struggled to achieve a note of wounded magnanimity.

'It was a long time ago.' Hoping to sound how he looked, Eliot tried to scrunch his features into a mask of nobly borne regret. There was no response, so he added, 'We were different people then.'

He still twinged with disbelief that she could hear him talk like that and not mind.

'Oh, I know I myself was different once. Don't try to deny it. But you never change, Eliot. I mean that in the very best sense … Oh and I know this might be a bit unlikely – but do you have any idea yet when you'll get down the river to London? … Oh, well, you know, it was just a vague thought …Oh… So you have got to Oxford today, like you said you would? …Oh, well …Yes…Byee. Bye for now…'

*

Something amiss? How could that be? thought Chris. On a day like this.

Lunch at his old college had not offered the untoothsome ordeal of roast swan, nor stuffed peacock with all the feathers put back on. On the contrary, each course, with accompanying vintage, had been good enough to qualify as what he'd once heard called a rocking-chair experience: one of those times whose memory you'd bring out in idle old age to dwell upon with total satisfaction. In a not-too-bad life, it had been suggested, a score of maybe twelve such occasions was pretty good.

The day itself had conspired in his well-being – the bright, calm weather and the sunlit city full of frolicking younger versions of himself and his friends, flitting about on foot or old bikes like the chorus in a comic opera. It was odd to see, as he rambled and mused, how little change the past quarter century had wrought in student fashions. There was still the same, often unisex, ensemble of white T-shirts, black leather and denim. As ever, many of the boys had made an if-not-now-when attempt at a beard; and the girls, in a similar spirit of once in a lifetime, wore smooth thick hair halfway to their waist. No change there.

Returning, he'd taken the long way round, the better to prolong his own contentment and pay his respects to a few favourite views of the place.

But then. In the long avenue through Christchurch Meadow to the river, any sense of starring in an upbeat movie of his own life was suddenly checked.

At first he couldn't tell what was wrong, though his hands and feet sweated as promptly as if a switch had been thrown, and his entrails felt about to warp. He examined himself: wallet not missing, flies done up. Then he looked around him, at what he knew to be one of the most urbane and unmenacing townscapes on earth. Nothing out of order there; cows grazed in the great Meadow, tourists lightly peopled the broad shady path to the Thames, and the towers of Merton and Magdalen stood where they ought, in a view unchanged since the Wars of the Roses.

Then, half fearful, half relieved, he spotted it. He was standing under an elm. All the other trees in the avenue were elms, too – even as he knew they couldn't be, not since the great insect-borne plague of a generation ago.

They'd been replaced since then, but with something else. Poplars, that was it.

Chris screwed his eyes shut, then opened them, on a vista still shaded by non-existent English elms. He sat down on a bench, and applied himself to what he saw, not just as a scholar but how he thought a scientist might do. Guessing – rightly – that his memory to this point was uncompromised, hypnosis could be ruled out as thoroughly as time travel. From there, it wasn't far to getting it more or less right: the blame lay with something he'd eaten. Never mind where or how; all that mattered now was getting back to the boat and into his bunk. Preferably without finding the streets jammed with horse-drawn cabs and carriers' carts, while getting jostled up against Matthew Arnold or scraping elbows with John Ruskin.

*

Two hours after being kindly received at the great College, and with his photos and notes completed, Eliot took a short cut back through Golden Fleece Lane towards the High.

What he saw there took him at first by surprise. He had forgotten, if he'd ever known, that this must be Encaenia Day. He'd read about it of course, sometime in his youth, when he was struggling to make a living amid the jealous ache of not having gone to university. This annual procession of all that was most dignified and flamboyant in Oxford's academic life had concentrated everything he felt about the place. Now, from inside Golden Fleece Lane on the steps of an ancient house converted to university offices, he was able to watch over the heads of the onlookers out on the High. Seen like this, as they passed the narrow byway's entrance the parading university members looked like figures on an animated frieze.

He was lucky: it looked as if the procession had only just reached his viewpoint. At its head walked the University Marshall, in a long velvet-caped coat and carrying a silver baton. Next, the University Chancellor, stepping out as though his long black robe, freighted with gold braid, must weigh no more than a stone or so. Its long train was carried by an undergraduate in evening dress.

By comparison the High Steward's cap and gown were scarcely medieval-bling at all. Supposedly he presided over some almost forgotten court that tried undergraduates for treason; a post that hadn't seen a pay rise, or even a spot of index-linking, for centuries. So, Eliot wondered, had he at least had his annual fee converted from old pennies to some new, legal tender?

The Doctors of the Faculties embodied the procession at its most gorgeous: Divinity, all robed in scarlet faced with black velvet and edged with yellow; Music, in brocaded cream satin with facings of crimson. The Proctors in black, faced with dark blue and yellow and red; each, at their back, with a long black silk hood turned inside out and lined with miniver …

*

'How did I do, Roly darling?' Marina had wanted to say on ringing off. Then she saw her son's face.

His handsome features wore a look of wretchedness such as she'd never imagined. She scarcely knew him: her Roly never, ever doubted himself.

'You know, darling, Eliot was really quite encouraging.'

'It didn't seem that way. Not from where I'm standing.' As if to himself he groaned, 'There must be something one can do!'

'I'm sure everything possible is in train. And it'll only be a few days. He said so himself.'

'But he didn't give a date, did he?' He stared through his mother and beyond with a frown of calculation.

'Well, yes, he did, darling. That time you met him.'

'I mean a sooner date!'

Marina willed herself not to catch his eye.

'But ... I mean, even if your firm is affected' – Roland currently worked at a grand West End car showroom – 'surely the redundancies wouldn't be that sudden. Besides I can't believe they won't see someone like you as indispensable.' Marina had forgotten how he hated it when she claimed to know anything about his world.

He evaded her imploring eyes. 'Let's not talk about it, okay? Let's just not say another word.' Swivelling back towards her, he exclaimed, 'But I need the money now!'

'What money, darling?'

'Don't ask – don't bother. Just don't ask!... I told you. I need them to get to London. I need a fucking date!'

As he left her over-furnished living room, then hurried from the tiny but expensive flat, Marina told herself he'd always been a sensitive boy, whose instinct for winning could sometimes weigh on him very hard indeed. It took a few moments to pull her thoughts together, at the end of which she recalled that this was one of the things she loved about her son.

Besides, his instinct for coming first had always made him exaggerate any setback. Darling Roly was just like her: he hated to lose. Knowing that about him was what made her feel he was still a part of herself ...

*

... As the Heads of Houses processed past him, Eliot, who prided himself on a memory for detail, found that, yes, he could remember which title, Warden or Master, Provost or President, went with which College. After the other Professors, and the Lecturers, Readers, and Fellows, the BA's followed; then the undergraduates. The Scholars had the relative dignity of knee-length gowns with bell sleeves. Chris, jammy sod, had been one of these. Compared to him Eliot figured that Mike, up here as a Commoner, was one of the academic hoi polloi. A group of these ordinary youths were passing now, in their frivolous-looking waist-length gowns, with the University Registrar bringing up the end of the procession. Blinking at the contrast between the sunlit High and the permanently shaded alley where he stood, Eliot had the sense of a warp in reality; it would hardly have surprised him if his two friends, miraculously restored to youth, had also paraded before him.

It felt, too, almost as if he'd once seen the rest of the

Encaenia ceremony himself, such was the clarity with which he pictured the procession's ending. In the Bodleian, the doors of the Tower of the Five Orders closing behind them. Then the crowded Sheldonian Theatre, the National Anthem, the speeches, mostly in Latin; and, finally, the Chancellor touching his black and gold mortarboard, before declaring, 'Dissolvimus hanc Convocationem.'

Could it be sunstroke? Back on the boat, he'd try and remember to wear a hat.

XII

...the most famous University of Oxford, our most
noble Athens, the seat of our English Muses,
the prop and the pillar, nay the sun, the eye
and the very soul of the nation, whence religion,
letters and good manners are plentifully diffused
through the whole kingdom...

William Camden (1551-1623)

Unlike the others, on setting out for Oxford that day Mike
had been uncertain what he should feel.

'Just catching up with someone – you know, touching
base.'

'Avoiding them, more like,' Eliot had murmured as
Mike left. Chris, ever circumspect, merely nodded as they
watched their friend resolutely striding away down the
towpath.

For days beforehand Mike had said nothing; whenever
he thought of this morning's venture he'd been surprised
by how unfriendly the ache of anticipation could be.

And yet. He was only going to look at an artwork; one
that he'd already seen, half completed in his son's studio.

He'd promised at the time that if need be he'd go out of his way to see the finished work. It was the least he could now do, from parental loyalty and personal pride alike.

He also needed to vanquish a small doubt, first raised by something Bianca had said. Several weeks ago, now.

'I think you have not heard yet from your grown-up family? Since they were informed about us?'

It was too soon, he'd told her, to see it like that.

But she'd persisted.

'Your – I mean, the person you were married to before. Perhaps she has told people' – meaning Mike's son and daughter – 'that they should not have contact with you.'

'Anna is an honourable person,' he'd heard himself say, as if declaiming from a script in bad translation. 'She would never do something like that.'

Bianca had suppressed a shrug and instead looked up at him earnestly. 'Oh, well. I'm sure they will get accustomed to things – I mean, used to things as they were always going to be.'

He'd put it out of mind that ever since he and Bianca had met he'd had no direct contact with his children. There'd just been his one carefully worded, almost courtly letter to Anna, in which he'd announced the great change in his life and respectfully insisted on a divorce. He'd also expressed gratitude for their years together, at the same time asking for her support in reaffirming the fatherly affection he would always feel towards Sam and Jessie.

The only response had come from Anna's lawyer, in the form of a neutral correspondence concerned solely with details of settlement. Meanwhile there was no word from their children, nor mention of them from anyone else.

Until, that was, the day when he and Bianca were married.

At the reception Bianca's mother had worn a frown of purpose like a knife between the eyes, as she scanned the heap of presents that for some reason had to go on show. ('This would please my family so much, Michael.')

Turning to him, she demanded, 'And those other people -?'

'Which other people?'

'Those other people who still think they have a claim on you. I can tell that they wish us to see how they have sent you no presents. No felicitous salutation card – nothing.'

To spare his bride further awkwardness, he'd turned away to greet another guest. Bianca meanwhile, speaking rapidly with her mother in their own language, was no doubt remonstrating. Whatever it was that she said, his heart had swelled in sympathy and admiration at her forbearance...

It wouldn't do to turn up too soon at the gallery. For various reasons Mike felt he'd rather view the exhibition as one of the public, even if there were, well, nobody there that he knew. He took a short detour through Radcliffe Square, but found it blocked at one end by crowd barriers. Corralled at a distance up a side street stood a group of animal-rights demonstrators; tirelessly they shouted slogans, with the persistence of a neighbour's dog fated to bark all night.

Of course: today was the Encaenia procession, or

what annually remained of it in the face of the protestors. Compared to what Mike remembered, it had been reduced in recent times to a notion of itself; any properly funded theme park would have done better. Rather than hundreds of University members parading down the High in every kind of full academic dress, a few dozen went by. Recognizing some famous faces from the wider world, Mike guessed that almost everyone present, wearing a vacationer's look of good cheer in their unaccustomed cap and gown, must be on the way to receive an honorary degree.

The route had shrunk too; it scarcely extended beyond one side of the great cobbled and pinnacled square, round to where the Divinity Schools' massive doors would close behind what little there was to see. A hundred or so spectators, also penned up, applauded and took photos; and in three or four minutes the procession had gone. Even so, it was surprising, come to think of it, not to see Eliot in the crowd.

For, whatever his friends' perceptions of the city, yesterday Mike had scoffed none of the foraged hallucinogen which, suddenly and unsuspected, was now turning their perceptions into burnished illusion.

It wasn't far to the gallery, in the former livery stable of a pub once called the Marquis of Granby but now, with half an eye on the tourist trade, re-named the Compleat Wrangler. Outside the broad, dim archway leading to the yard, a large poster advertised the exhibition. Mike, preoccupied, collided in the entrance with someone he'd come to think of as almost family: his daughter's long-term boyfriend. Or should that be partner?

'Ben!' he said.

'Oh!' said Ben. Who suddenly looked anxious. Almost as if one of them shouldn't be there.

Both men simultaneously blurted, How are you? Hurriedly Mike added, 'I mean both of you, of course – how's Jessie?'

For some reason Ben looked shifty; he even blushed. For a dark-haired man he had a very fair, transparent skin, which at moments still evoked the small choirboy he'd been when as classmates he and Sam had formed their enduring friendship.

The younger man's awkwardness prompted a suspicion in Mike, who said, 'I know it's not entirely my business … but are things well between you both?' For some reason he felt a rush of unease; it was only young Ben's inability to meet his eye that helped him speak with his usual directness.

'No, everything's fine.' Ben hesitated, like a drunk who pauses before going ahead anyway with an indiscretion. 'I mean – I should say – things are excellent.'

His look of holding something back was unmistakable. Mike was led to say, 'Uh … weren't you thinking of getting married? I mean, or' – stumbling in a way he never did – 'maybe I misremembered. And after all, people change their minds about these things, all the time …' Uneasily he recalled that he and Ben hadn't met since the alteration in his own married life.

'Oh, no – no, that's still on. Very much so.'

For a man announcing his engagement of marriage before a prospective father-in-law, Ben showed not the faintest gleam of gladness. All the way from childhood, Mike remembered, he'd been incapable of lying. Right now, tensed and apprehensive, he looked ready to turn aside and flee.

'Well, Ben, that's splendid,' Mike ventured. At such a moment one had a duty to say something upbeat about marriage. Indeed the words 'I hope you'll both be as happy together as we always –' came within a pico-second of parading carelessly off the end of his tongue.

Still needing to probe, he managed to say, 'I know I've been a bit hard to get hold of recently. I hope you weren't concerned about, uh, speaking to me first before asking Jessie. Or any of that stuff. I mean, nobody does that nowadays … Er … do they? No – no; of course they don't…'

Ben started to hasten away. 'Well, I'm glad I've had this chance to mention it … Goodbye –'

'But no – wait – when are you and Jessie announcing a date?'

Half-turned to go, Ben looked troubled and evasive.

'And how soon do you plan to send out invitations? If you and Jessie haven't got my current address, I can give it to you now. It must be good for … oh, several months yet.' He started to fumble in his pockets.

His daughter's soon-to-be husband looked on at him, no longer with embarrassment so much as anxious resolve. Ben was thinking how, if he didn't immediately tell Jessie's father the truth about their wedding plans, he risked making the job fall to her. No way was that to be thought of.

'Yes,' Ben said, 'do please send me your address. But I think – well, I know – Jessie would want me to tell you – the invitations have already gone out.'

Mike forced a smile of reassurance. 'Well, look, that's no problem. You know I'd cancel anything to play my part.'

He meant giving Jessie away, if it was that sort of wedding. Though somehow he couldn't say so right out.

'When is the date you've fixed? And have you chosen a venue?' An unpleasant thought occurred to him. Facing it down, he said, 'I won't bring my – Bianca needn't be there, if you'd rather not.'

This time Ben did look him in the eye. Mike couldn't miss how the younger man's face was overcast with pity.

'It's in London. By Smithfield. At St Bartholomew the Great. The date –'

'Good God! That is impressive. But for a place like that, don't you have to book a long time in advance?'

'Well, yes.'

'Oh… But – you were about to say – the date is when?' Ben told him.

Before Mike was capable of responding, he added, 'We did know you'd planned to be on holiday at the time – on the river …'

Mike stopped him with a gesture. 'No – please.' After a pause he asked, 'Now that we've actually met like this, is there anything else I should know?'

Before Ben could answer he cut in with the truth it seemed one of them must utter.

'Jessie doesn't want me there.'

It was more easily said as a statement than a question.

Ben saw that any hint of kindness would be intolerable. 'She didn't actually say that. Only I think – I mean, I know – your name isn't on the guest list.'

Mike turned away, then back. He looked less resolute than at any time since he was eight years old.

At length he demanded, 'Is anyone giving her away?'

Seeing him more grieved than wrathful, Ben nonetheless answered warily.

'Jessie's uncle Angus is going to do it.'

Anna's elder brother. It was he who'd introduced her to Mike. In the pub, after a university rugger match.

There was nothing more to be said. At least, nothing that would make things better.

Parting in other circumstances from his son-in-law-to-be, Mike would have shaken hands, with heartfelt brusque goodwill. As it was, he could only venture a bodged-up wave of farewell, before turning away into the shadow of the gallery entrance.

XIII

*[Jude fell] into thought on what struggling
people like himself had stood at the Crossway,
whom nobody ever thought of now. It had more
history than the oldest college in the city. It was
...teeming, stratified, with the shades of human
groups, who had met there for tragedy, comedy,
farce; real enactments of the intensest kind...
Here the two sexes had met for loving, hating,
coupling, parting; had waited, had suffered,
for each other; had triumphed over each other;
cursed each other in jealousy, blessed each other
in forgiveness...*

Jude the Obscure, Thomas Hardy, 1896

The river has little to do with most of Oxford. Around
the Ferret and Fishcake pub, a neighbourhood of flood-
prone Victorian terraces now houses few working men;
stonemasons and brewery workers have been replaced
by over-stretched postgraduate couples knocking away at
preferment's door. It lies near a formerly squalid waterfront
once mentioned by guidebooks with shuddering

disrespect for its soap-works, sawmill and coal-yards but since transformed into a neat townscape of glass balconies and landscaped young shrubbery.

Downriver past the town's main bridge, the Thames broadens, loosed into a landscape of sports fields and water meadows. Here, on the terrace of a waterside pub close to the flow of traffic under and over Folly Bridge, while Eliot and his friends were each preoccupied elsewhere, two men waited. Though they sat at a table among a multitude of tourist nationalities, they themselves had nothing to do with the world of organized leisure. Dressed casual smart, lounging but alert, they wore a look of work-day purpose. One, consulting his phone, eventually found the image he'd been seeking. With a wordless perfunctory glance at the other man, he passed it over, the better for them to recognize the *Speedwell* once she emerged from under the bridge.

'That should do...'

'If this shit exists.'

'...for now.'

*

Mike paid his entrance fee and went into the gallery. When the Compleat Wrangler was still an important coaching inn this building, with its stone floor and exposed-brick walls, had housed enough horseflesh to warm itself on nothing but dung-smelling body heat. For the purpose of the exhibition it had space enough to be partitioned into a series of enclosures. The venue was quite crowded for a show put on by a group of young artists just starting out; and at first Mike wasn't sure where to find the piece he'd come to see.

The scene outside with Jessie's lover, soon to be her husband, receded. It did so because he willed it that way. All his life Mike had known how to make his powers of attention march in step with what he wanted; to wheel about and take precise aim just as he thought they should. Yes, he was heartsick at what he'd just learned. But he was also a grown man, and a soldier who'd faced losses in the field and learned to cope by focusing immediately upon whatever else came next.

At the door he bought a catalogue of the works on show, and zipped it into his pocket for later, as a souvenir of this stage in Sam's career.

He had a fair idea of how Sam's sculpture should look: his son, full of enthusiasm back at the outset, had emailed preliminary sketches showing life-size figures memorialized in effigy.

'Some berk's bound to call it iconoclastic. But seriously, Dad, that just means it'll be true to life. You'll like it – if it comes out right.'

It had to be the item furthest from the entrance, at that moment hidden by a group of people, where a spotlight on a ceiling track lit something freestanding. Mike went towards it, as the other onlookers moved away.

He found himself standing alone before an image that in his own opinion counted as obscene.

You could see how the work had turned out like this. At first, all Sam must have wanted was to vary the style of medieval tomb on which husband and wife traditionally lay side by side in an attitude of piety. Here, instead of each facing upwards, hands together in prayer, or looking dignified while leaning on one elbow, the two figures must have been planned to look like any couple sitting up in bed first thing in the morning. She was drinking a cup of coffee and he was making a phone call. At their feet, in place of the traditional crouching hound a cat was curled up asleep. Modelled presumably on Watchit, the family's tabby, whose idea of bliss had been to have his tail vanish up a vacuum cleaner.

So far, so predictable. But since this middle-aged couple had been based on everyday life, at some point personal resemblances were bound to take over. The woman, at least, was still a good likeness.

Of Anna, naturally. Even amid the unfolding revelations of a moment like this, Mike, who understood little of art and its processes, was impressed at what could be done with – what had Sam said? – a frame of chicken wire covered in painted papier mâché. The wig, a shining cap of auburn hair or whatever, couldn't have been more lifelike. He even fancied that their son had caught a certain look of hers, in which repose mingled with responsiveness.

The other figure of course, newspaper in one hand, phone in the other, must at some stage have been Mike himself.

Not any more.

It now featured a giant frog's head. Beneath a confetti-dredged topper the creature's mouth was clamped fast on a large artificial rose, stained and dismembered, its petals mostly fallen. An inscription in Gothic lettering, presumably moulded from fibreglass, bristled across the side of the tomb: 'Requiescat in pace Amor'. More wording was spray-painted across this, graffito-style. 'Methinks I was enamoured,' read one scrawl, and another, 'Reader, I kissed him.'

Confronted by a truth that nothing could finesse away, all Mike felt at that moment was a faint disorientation. In vain he wished some merely physical harm had clobbered him, and made him hallucinate all this.

'You have to give this piece credit, as a spirited offering. Wouldn't you say?'

'What?'

The man who'd spoken was an agreeable-looking fellow in his sixties, tall and strongly built, with an air of academic honours urbanely borne. Taking advantage of the free speech between strangers you sometimes get in such a place, he added, 'But don't you think it's been contrived for the satisfaction of the artist rather than his public? Whatever the story behind it.'

No matter that in all his adult life Mike had never been so unpunctilious. Without a word he turned, and walked away.

*

Where, though, was there left for a man to go at such a time? In Mike's case the answer had to be a few hundred yards away, at his old college. It wasn't a conscious choice, but the destination was obvious, as somewhere he could escape backwards in time. Outside time, almost. Never mind that every pragmatic impulse ran counter to such illusion. In the sealed sub-basement of his mind it would still have been hard for him to imagine a point in history when the arcaded gravitas of Front Quad or the weathered stone dormers of Candlemass Quad had not existed – when this piece of ground might have been only a mulberry orchard or a muddy archery range.

The college building standing farthest from the Porter's Lodge and the world outside was the library. As a place to keep books it was only a few years old; as a building it was one of the most ancient in all of Oxford, a deconsecrated Anglo-Saxon church known as St Eanswythe within the Walls. From outside it appeared as crude as an early industrial engine house. Inside, its undulating stone floor, small deep windows and massive walls made the library's furnishings and lighting look as if they'd invaded a cavern hacked from the living rock. Mike went and sat down at one of the long desks where he'd used to sit and work as an undergraduate.

Here was where he'd been free. It was a feeling, more than a fully shaped thought. In this place every large decision of his life, with any later justification duly hauled into place, had been somewhere off in a vague future that shone like early mist in midsummer. Coming up here for his first term, high on unfocused hope, was like being a newborn, only armed with the knowledge and freedom of a grown man. No doubts nor fears; not one nagging dishevelled passion.

He clasped his hands behind his head, unthinkingly

mimicking an attitude of his younger self, and looked up into the vaulted shadows of the roof. In the last hour enough had befallen him to make every ordinary thing he saw or heard scrape against his consciousness like an unbearable minor assault. The large dimness above him was a refuge, where nothing could have changed.

It had, though. High on the former chancel arch there'd been restoration work. He recognized the small primitive figure immediately; it had always enjoyed notoriety, especially among the young gentlemen of the College. The Victorians had claimed to think, in a truly impressive misunderstanding of anatomy, that it was a pious image of the exposed Sacred Heart. She – for this was a she like nothing else – had formerly been outside, above the south door; but like so many of the city's decaying gargoyles and imperial heads, doubtless she'd been threatened by traffic pollution.

So at more than a thousand years old she'd been brought indoors for her own protection. A small spotlight was carefully trained on her Dark Age bug eyes and her poorly made arms, carved by someone who couldn't do elbows, as she hitched them under her knees. To heave open, not any old quim, but what must surely have been meant as the largest vaginal orifice in the world. You were probably supposed to imagine whole nations issuing out of it, whether tumbling as if from a cornucopia or marching forth in files.

A man could go in there, Mike thought, and his friends and family would never hear of him again.

He looked up at the thing, hang-dog as any confused

creature. For a moment he was tempted to rail inwardly against whatever antiquarian-minded convocation of prats had voted to put it there. Right there, in his very own prospective line of sight.

Then he stood up, casting off self-pity as a valiant man should. As if responding to a bark of command he turned and strode from the building, determined that not a minute more should be lost. With him at the wheel of the boat, by evening they could surely be clear of Folly Bridge, and away from this town.

XIV

'I love history, especially the bits from the olden days, like here...'

'I hate history. Why couldn't we go to Orlando...?'

'Have many people noticed that Sir James's portrait is a reproduction? It's been flopped, so that he's looking the wrong way...'

'Who is this would-be pedant writing in green ink? Sir James has been flopped so that he's facing his wife, as one of a pair. And no one expects to see originals...'

'Has anybody else spotted the trompe l'oeil in the stable yard? The one made of seashells? We did, on our first day...'

Visitors' Book at Crickley Old Deanery, near Oxford

What you saw depended on where you were, as the *Speedwell* passed under the bridge. A pigeon fouling a niche below the parapet, or a tourist pausing two metres above, would have seen the boat glide forth beneath them, together with the top side of Monty, ears and tail flowing in the wind as he strained forward in the prow like a naval figurehead, bound under divine protection into victorious combat.

From the deck the gleam of the river by Christchurch Meadow, and the hot countryside beyond, were all the more brilliant for having been framed within the bridge's dark arch.

Seen from the riverbank, where the two men outside the pub were waiting even now, the arch's reflection gave the illusion of a complete circle, above and below the surface of the water, from whose very centre the boat emerged. For an instant the *Speedwell* seemed supported by nothing, as her superstructure and the figures on board converted from silhouettes to full colour.

This effect made no impression on the two unsuspected watchers, though nobody could have looked on more intently. They'd not worked together before; yet they were as sparing in word and gesture as any dour married couple of fifty years' standing. Looking on with neutral professionalism at the passing boat, again they handed the phone and its image one to the other; then with purpose but no haste they got up and left.

With Mike at the helm the *Speedwell* surged downriver at topmost legal speed. In the galley Chris paused to neck down a judicious torrent of tap water in his quest for a return to reality. He glanced warily out of a porthole: if one side of the great Meadow had been shaded by elms that weren't there, would its riverbank also be lined with long-gone College barges? With their balustraded roofs crowded by Edwardians, dressed for Eights Week with pedantic extravagance, down to the last valeted boot-button or ivory-handled parasol? He braced himself, saw nothing, and dared to hope that for the rest of the day nothing would befall him that held the smallest interest.

Only where they passed beneath the main line to London did he suffer a few moments more of queasy apprehension. Through the window by his bunk he saw a train pass above them. Oh, God, no. Steam-powered – no, seriously … A four-six-nought King class, shining and resplendent in the green-and-gold livery of the GWR, God's Wonderful Railway …

It was the clarity and brightness of the colours that brought him back to himself, with an almost equal shock of relief. Chris was too young to have seen the abolition of the age of steam. But he did remember Uncle Hugh telling him what a surprise it had been when in honour of the Coronation all the mainline engines were cleaned, so that what had seemed to have left the foundry in matt black now gleamed as many-splendored as Thomas the Tank Engine and his friends.

He realized too that the carriages were not only the wrong colours; they weren't the right date. No proper old-style corridor compartments here, with half-tone photos advising you to visit some seaside resort long since semi-derelict. Before the train was out of sight the look of its passengers had told all: three hundred grey-haired men in the comfortable dun-coloured clothes of early retirement, plus nearly half that number of wives, on a luncheon-special day trip into their own past.

Some of them waved down at the two or three boats visible from the bridge. Eliot, lounging in a chair on deck, waved back, all of them for that moment bright-eyed boys again.

That evening the *Speedwell* moored early; they were due next day to accept an invitation issued by Leonora to some form of lunch party just down-river. All Chris had had, a few days before, was a call on his mobile – but then even his aunt's phone calls could sound embossed and deckle-edged.

'Do tell your friends you're to come just as you are, won't you, Crispin darling. It'll be perfect, having you all just drop by at our informal fête champêtre. Straight from your wonderful boat.'

'Informal my arse,' he'd thought. Ever the loyal foster-child, Chris would never have said such a thing out loud. Where Leonora was concerned, only within his subconscious did the honest sceptic in him peep forth. All the same, at the sound of her voice he'd unwittingly put on the look, uncommitted but benign, with which he heard out his worst students' essays. Instinct reminded him that, forceful or not, as a social creature Leonora could pick up on shades of meaning scarcely more plangent than the beat of a moth's wing.

'And there'll be lovely friends of mine who happen to be filming in the area this week; it'll be an opportunity for you to meet some splendidly interesting people...'

'Excellent,' he'd murmured, as his aunt laid a table before his mind's eye where he and his mates might feast and quaff alongside some of her most valued contacts.

So. Aboard the *Speedwell*, tomorrow morning would bring the call for each of them to put on a clean shirt and a clear mind. After they'd moored, Mike got into the dinghy and was straining to surpass his usual distance. Eliot, likewise seeking exercise, volunteered to take Monty on a mile or so's snufflefest of towpath undergrowth.

Chris sat on deck, in the evening's lingering tender light, and frowned with concentration at the screen glowing on his lap.

'...Dare I ask, Crispin dear: how is Hugh's eulogy coming along?'...

That had been some days ago, when a truthful answer was still not too embarrassing.

'Just trying out different openings, Leonora. You know how it is. Got to get this bit right at least.'

Hoping a pixel's worth of inspiration might glint out from somewhere, he returned to his download of Leonora's recent documentary. Again he set himself to study every word, as the commentary described how his aunt's experience of marriage and motherhood had intertwined with her public career in journalism, advising the nation's poor in spirit how to fix themselves.

He looked again at the touching sequence where she sat beneath the little canvas pavilion in the spacious garden of their weekend home, with Uncle Hugh's empty chair evoking his death and the end of their long, much-publicised marriage. This segued into mention of another, earlier loss, as the screen filled with a photograph of Imogen looking withdrawn and unreadable.

Leonora's voice said, 'Because mental illness is often a

mystery, that doesn't mean it should be hidden away and not discussed. Besides, how could I justly face all those readers who ask me for help, if I myself hadn't shared some of their troubles. It means much to me, to know that I have found within myself resources of strength whose existence I'd never suspected, even as I set aside the hopes her father and I once had for our daughter.

'And now that my much loved husband is dead, I can be forgiven for saying that it was he who most found our adored daughter's condition so hard to bear. But however much she distressed him, I would be the last to say she deserves any blame. For not trying harder, I mean, to make some sort of recovery ...'

There was nothing here to help with his speech. Stiff with frustration and moving slowly, like an explorer on a heavy-gravity planet, Chris got to his feet, to allow himself a break while walking up and down the towpath and touching base with a call to Martha.

He described tomorrow's party, complete with gossipy details of how he imagined it. 'You're all word-pictures, aren't you?' Tom had once said, overhearing such a conversation between them. 'Like a cartoon strip made for radio.'

'Will Imogen be there?' Martha asked, thinking of his cousin's seeming improvement.

'I don't think so.'

Unwary for once, she couldn't help edging onto forbidden ground.

'Have we ever seen her together with Leonora? I mean, since what her mother calls "this condition of hers"?'

'I don't know why either of us should need to ask a question like that,' he answered, with a brusqueness that the world at large would never have recognized. 'No one has a right to think my cousin is being kept at arm's length, least of all by her own mother.'

Martha had known to say nothing almost before she'd spoken. Quickly she retreated towards safety, with some remark about Leonora's every word and deed coming from bewilderment at her daughter's disordered mind, and the grief of bereavement. From there she changed the subject, so that by the time Eliot returned with Monty, who was all burrs in his coat, filthy and happy, both she and Chris were restored to their usual selves. From where he was sluicing Monty down at the water's edge, Eliot could hear Chris's even-tenored voice shifting in and out of earshot as he strolled back and forth. Even when the words were indistinguishable Eliot could tell from his tone who his friend was talking to.

'… No one's gone mad …' You could hear the smile in Chris's voice. ' … And you and I still don't hate each other…' He guffawed conspiratorially at something Martha must have said. Eliot had known Martha almost as long as Chris had; so he could tell that she too must be laughing.

Other much-divorced men might have resented some of their married friends' habitual good cheer, with an inward mutter of, Why not me too? But Eliot's mishaps in marriage had all come from good intentions, and it was something of the same unthinking generosity that made him ask, 'Well, why not them, rather than me?'

No such thought was in Mike's mind, when he came back on board. Why should it be? A hard-won sweat plus the lapse of several hours had dulled, if not exorcised, the day's untoward moments back in Oxford. No doubt there was little that couldn't eventually be explained and smoothed over. Meanwhile no man in his position had cause to be jealous of anyone's marriage, since he, fearless and resolute, had done exactly what he wanted; and once this brief holiday from life was over, he and Bianca would have nothing more to do with their shared thereafter but be perfectly happy …

*

The Old Deanery's garden was a scene blessed with perfect light and shade. The half-acre lawn was cropped to a moleskin smoothness that seemed scarcely achievable without laying a pair of nail scissors to every blade of grass.

And yes, there were film people. 'You know each other, of course,' said Leonora, doing the introductions. She wore summery clothes that contrived to be both shapeless and elegant, with a broad-brimmed straw hat.

'Indeed we do,' said Chris, promptly and with a firm handshake to hide any shortfall of delight. He and his friends had more or less anticipated the presence of Cressida, as a former colleague of Leonora, together with Shitty Jerry.

'Still a free man, huh?' the latter said to Mike. 'While you're still here on the river, at least.'

'Ah, your wonderful boat,' cried Leonora, not

understanding, but acute enough to sense some form of tension. 'You must show us over it,' she told Eliot, 'after we've had lunch. But now …' She turned, poised for more introductions; meanwhile Eliot, whose general goodwill made him apt at remembering personal details, asked, 'It's Imogen's birthday, isn't it? Is she here?'

Leonora missed half a beat, then said, 'I wanted something more personal for her. That's why the birthday party is fixed just for her, in a few days from now. Down the river, at the perfect place. If you're all free, that would make it even more wonderful…'

The dozen other guests, grouped drink in hand, were chatting in front of the late-medieval Deanery, with its look of having been somehow detached from one of the Colleges just up-river. The house belonged to a public Trust which restored antique buildings to rent out as expensive holiday lets. Leonora had taken it for a fortnight; and helped by her omnipresent PA and numerous caterers she was staging a dense succession of parties, picnics and dinners whose organization and hosting would have felled a lesser woman. She relished her flair for being lavish and hospitable, and her enjoyment was readily shared by her guests. Usually, too, she assembled her invitation lists with the care of a craftsman; Chris wondered what hidden agendas today's seating plan might reveal.

Naught for Mike's comfort; that was soon plain. On a long outdoor table, canopied against the sun and extravagantly set as if framed up for a TV advertisement, he found himself across the table from Cressida. The siren witch who'd lured away Bianca's husband and left her and their babies defenceless before the world.

As if to fuel Mike's squeamish upright disdain, Cressida was describing for comic effect the time a previous live-in boyfriend had accepted an afternoon's custody of his seven-year-old daughter.

'Do you know what she did? She wanted to marry me! We had to go through this whole ceremony thing together. And then –' Cressida paused, to suppress a laugh – 'you won't believe this, but she made me do it all over again – four times!'

'You must have been a hero,' put in Jerry from down the table.

'I was, too! Though, afterwards I thought I shouldn't have done that – humouring a dishonest fantasy. How is anyone to get on with their life if they don't face facts…?'

The tall, grey-haired man placed at Leonora's right looked and listened intently, but gave no response. He'd been introduced to Chris as a professor of psychiatry, though without mention of the fact that he'd just taken responsibility for Imogen's case.

Leonora turned the talk to families in general and the mystery of childrens' personal development. Largely, as Chris suspected, to draw out her neighbour the professor, whom she treated with a deference he'd never seen in her before. From there she moved on to stage and film characterisations, in an attempt simultaneously to engage her other neighbour. This was one of the cast members starring in *Zuleika Dobson*, presumably seated next to Leonora as one of her two most honoured guests. The actor, an agreeable-seeming chap who worked under his own name of Edmund ...Fazackerley, was it ... must have kept his unstarry moniker either to stand out, or from utter confidence in his prospects. Chris had seen him on screen already, as a comic-book superdude similar to his present role. As someone who'd never even been in a school play, he marvelled at how different the guy looked while being himself: no longer a spoof patrician, more a borderline-dumpy Everyman.

As talk turned to the movie, manners or modesty made Fazackerley reluctant to hold forth about his own contribution. Not so Cressida.

'I've been writing Zuleika from the heart and guts of my own self,' she declared. Animation became her. Chris, more sceptical than some, looked at her expressive violet eyes and delicately flushed skin and wondered if certain people had the gift of fine-tuning their physical appearance spontaneously, by will power.

'Not that I mean,' laughing to show self-deprecation, 'that whole crowds have ever fallen in love with me!'

It wasn't intended as much of a denial. From his place at the opposite end of the table from Leonora – 'You're the man of the family now, Crispin darling' – Chris noticed how any meaning in what Cressida said counted for little beside the awful power of how she said it. He'd once had a colleague like her, who could render strong men foolish with ingratiation just by the way she breathed forth such utterances as, 'forms in triplicate' or 'unsegmenting the landscape of the digital conversation to drive footfall more holistically'. Right now the psychology professor's teenage son, invited as a mark of respect for his parents, was gazing at Cressida with an admiration through which her actual words fell ignored like so many small dead things.

' …What I mean, is, I'm making her the embodiment of truth to one's own passions. As I have her say in the closing sequence, "Loyalty to your own personal future is all you need, as an individual standing up proud and faithful to yourself."'

Meanwhile Mike appeared to concentrate hard on his coronation chicken, like a surgeon calculating the primary incision in an untried critical procedure. In fact he was striving to forget that, last time he'd heard such things, he'd been declaring them to Bianca. Carefully, as if shifting something aside with the edge of his shoe, he nudged away the possibility that he may even have had a certain unaffordable diamond and sapphire ring in his pocket, boxed up in readiness.

Hold fast to this one thought, he told himself: if Faecal Jerry and his new consort had been put on this earth for any purpose, it was to assure him, Major Michael Caldicott MC, that he and they had nothing in common. Would he have deserted two young children? The very thought made his contemptuous inner self flare its nostrils like a seventeen-hand stallion.

From there, chewing slowly as if each mouthful were a thought to be digested, he moved on to persuade himself that his children – his adult children, to whom he'd always given his best and finest self – well, they wouldn't always be as angry with him as they seemed to think they were. Not permanently. Not once they stopped to consider. To contrast him as a father against … well, one or two others.

Cressida prattled on. Around the beautiful garden and throughout the fields and woods of Oxfordshire near and far, the birdsong of early summer was loud in the land. From the top of a massive weeping willow by the river the season's last cuckoo sounded; Leonora delightedly pointed it out, as if she'd contrived its presence herself. Chris wondered if its plumage marked it as female: an avian villainess. In a stand of rushes nearby, its offspring might even now be displacing a nestful of fledgling reed warblers; or if in a country hedgerow, a partly hatched clutch of dunnocks. Or perhaps, by a cornfield up on the downs, the eggs of a pair of yellowhammers might just have been seen off.

Coffee was served at tables scattered about the garden, under giant sunshades and in a splendid topiary arbour. It was a chance for Chris to talk in private with the psychiatrist, Professor Wetherly.

'Ah, Leonora's son! – Well, yes, not in the legal sense –' with a gesture of acknowledgement, coffee spoon in hand. 'But she does speak of you as the other man in her life. Her main source of support, after her recent bereavement.'

Though his words might have come from Leonora's mouth, Wetherly's manner suggested a certain massive economy in most things he said. Chris sometimes tried for the same effect, in lecture halls and tricky departmental meetings.

He answered the professor with something grateful, and tried not to look surprised at such praise. Whatever wholehearted sympathy he'd shown his aunt, he was buggered if this sounded quite like him. Guiltily he resolved that whatever Leonora wanted from him beyond a cracking good speech in church next week, he'd try harder to oblige.

'Your aunt went so far as to say that her daughter has more of a bond with you than with any other family member.'

Chris met the other man's steady professional look, with a sense of needing to weigh his own words. 'Well...' frowning with concentration ... 'with her late father, surely... What I mean is, no one could have been more attentive to her than he was. Especially in her turbulent teens. And the care he showed me...' He gestured, ineffectually. Gratitude to his foster parents was almost the only thing that rendered him inarticulate.

Professor Wetherly kept his gaze focused. 'How would you describe your cousin's reaction to her father's death?'

Chris mentioned his enforced absence overseas, adding, 'Devastated, surely ...?'

The professor gave no immediate response, then said, 'Forgive me for pressing you like this...' Wetherly was new to the case, Chris remembered... 'But the observations of the nearest relative – as your aunt in some sense considers you – can often be helpful, as something to set alongside the existing record...'

Chris started to answer with what, surely, was obvious. His uncle, better placed than anyone, had taken charge of Imogen's case, supported by two well-regarded subordinates who'd worked with him for years –

But here, with one deft swoop Leonora accosted them.

'Crispin darling, I hope you're not making Marcus talk

about work. I only invited him so that we could all enjoy each others' company. Both of you now, come and join us over here...'

They moved away, closer to the sounds of partying laughter and chat. Behind them the willow tree rustled and swayed like a prima ballerina. The cuckoo went on calling.

X V

Chris's indignant exit from the world of film had not silenced him as a writer, just yet.

And Everyman–who–is–called–Kenny came at last to Cumnor Hill. There by the roadside he espied a strange figure sitting pensive in a concrete bus shelter with a lap full of windflowers, wild hyacinths and early purple orchids. Strange, that is, as in outlandish, with an old–fashioned hat and a long grey cloak; yet somehow familiar.

'Excuse me,' said Kenny. 'I hope you don't mind me asking. But do I know you?'

'Most people do,' said the stranger.

'Most people?'

'Depending of course on how you define any sub–set of individuals thus described.'

'But ... I mean, the way you look ... Are you ...could you be ... Lob–lie–by–the–fire, Jack Cade, poor Jack of every trade, or Robin–run–by–the–wall, Ragged Robin, or one of the lords of No man's Land, good Lot – ?'

'Knock it off – '

'Well, yes, I suppose you don't talk like you were one of them. In fact, if you don't mind me saying so, you sound more like, uh, a college drop-out...'

'Of course I sound like a drop-out, you berk. I'm the bleeding Scholar Gypsy, innit?'

'Waiting for a bus?'

'Why should I be waiting for a bus? What would a ghost want with one of them? But I've got to sit somewhere, now all your shy retreats and distant bowers have copped it. Bricked over with sodding dream homes. At least I'm not expected to keep myself clean. How would you like it, performing your ablutions in a fucking bird bath?'...

Untitled work-in-progress by Dr Chris Lovell,
writing as Hercule Smogg

Different soils can grow different buildings, like a crop. So Chris thought, leaning on his pedals as he cycled uphill towards an appointment next day with Professor Wetherly. When the *Speedwell* had embarked from Lechlade on its voyage to town, it did so in a countryside of once-pauperised hamlets built from weathered pale limestone. A few days more would bring them to a chalky landscape of steep, soft-contoured downs with hanging woods above villages of timber-framing, knapped flint, and muted red-and-silver brick. Here beyond Oxford, among pine trees, and sandy lanes become suburban byways, what this otherwise infertile hilltop had produced, was Edwardian villas and private tennis courts.

Imogen's new place of refuge was in one of these mansions, where electric bells had once meant ultimate modernity and the garage, with chauffeur's quarters upstairs, had been a solid little dwelling in its own right, crowned by an elaborate weathervane. The main house, built for a famous poet of the day, had been extended in modern times with two new wings and all the institutional business of service areas and parking bays.

Inside was clean and light and spacious: comfortable enough, it seemed to Chris, even compared to the last place, which, let's face it, had been stately. And so it should have been, Martha had said, given the fees. Todingdon Hall had had a view of parkland within a wall four miles around. Its principal rooms featured the kind of marble fireplaces that, without a proper security contract, risked being lifted in the night for sale overseas by professionals working to order. Even the gazebo, as Leonora had pointed out, was listed Schedule A.

'…And yet she's still not happy …'

'What exactly does Imogen's mother mean by that?' Martha had asked.

Frowning, and harshened by foster-filial loyalty, Chris had snapped, 'What Leonora means is that on her daughter's account she's mystified and broken-hearted. Now and always. However hard she tries to hide it.'

He wore the same frown now in the consulting room, plus a thousand-yard stare out of the window while he heard what Wetherly had to say. Imogen herself was out that afternoon, on a routine visit to the dentist. As the encounter unfolded, Chris could have passed for the suspect of a fearful crime, withholding everything he still could.

'...If we may, I'd like to talk about the treatment, before considering the nature of your cousin's actual condition...'

*

On the river two hours later, having beaten Mike to the *Speedwell*'s dinghy, Chris was straining at the oars as if the pain of physical striving was all he could bear.

'... Would you say,' Wetherly had asked, 'that you yourself have noticed any recent improvement in Imogen's state of mind...?'

Chris had recognized the angling for spontaneous answers that he himself used in seminars. It did nothing to ease his growing anger and confusion.

He rowed on, scarcely caring whether some water-borne gin palace might thrust itself up out of the early-evening mist and plough him under.

'...Well, since you yourself say that on the lower dose your cousin shows signs of recovery, might you agree that this medication should be stopped altogether?'

Chris had said something defensive about not being a pharmacologist. As if buying time.

Wetherly was not going to be deflected. 'Yes; but might

you consider whether the original prescription was itself inappropriate?… No, I do concede that this wouldn't necessarily reflect on your uncle's judgement as a doctor; nor even on his motive…'

'Bloody man!' Chris said aloud, missing the water with his starboard oar. He lurched backwards, a figure of indignity. Scrabbling to recover the oar he added, 'Overbearing fucker!'

… He'd countered Wetherly with untypical sarcasm.

'Seriously? You take the view that my cousin's own father was simply prescribing the so-called liquid cosh? And leaving it at that?'

Faced with deliberate silence from Wetherly, at that moment even he couldn't avoid blustering.

'Is that really what you think should be expected? From a man of my uncle's professional standing?'

Eventually, not dropping his gaze, Wetherly replied, 'Before we go further, can you recall if, when your cousin became ill, you yourself were present? … Were you on hand when your cousin was originally referred?'

If the Professor's questioning was implacable, he did try to soften his manner. All this was lost on Chris, who hadn't felt such obliterating anger since he was an adolescent, bewildered at being suddenly motherless, then fatherless, and flinching at every grown-up expression of kindness…

He hadn't stood up and strode from the consulting room; much less slammed the door behind him with the Professor in mid-sentence. Truth to self in the form of unthinking good manners, plus some advancing thing he

dared not name, had kept him sitting there. Never mind
that his usual self, known to the world as a fair-minded
man of broad understanding, had momentarily ceased
to exist. For reasons he'd ignored, Chris recalled the time
when, skiing alone, he'd blundered off-piste in an area of
pine forest. Suddenly, sounds close by had signalled the
start of an avalanche. Small runnels of loose snow were
swirling past: in themselves, nothing. Below, he could just
make out the end of the trees, before a cloud of fine snow
closed on him like smoke. The noise must have ranked
with the split-you-down-the-middle din of heavy artillery.
Only when it stopped did he see how close he'd been.
Two metres away a severed tree trunk had hurtled past,
not arcing like a tossed caber, but shot like a monstrous
harpoon...

His habits of courtesy had held to the end; parting
from Wetherly, he'd astonished himself by shaking hands
as if nothing important had been said. Back on the misty
river, rowing as if in flight from something unnameable,
the worst of it was that with each mile cursing gave less
relief. Why foul his mouth, Chris thought, finally resting
on the oars, when his heart wasn't in it? Nor even his
spleen, come to that.

Yet snatches of what had been said kept rising to the
surface of his mind like a gaseous poison. Worst perhaps
was the shrillness, as he perceived it, of his own protests.

'...But Imogen was adored by her father. When she
was little he was –' With the beginnings of horror, Chris
had stopped himself just in time from saying, '...all over
her...'

So, now.

Aching throughout his body and beyond, he started rowing again, going scarcely faster than the current. By the time he reached the rendezvous at the pub where the *Speedwell* had moored at least he felt all choices had been taken from him. Out of loyalty to his broken-winged cousin he had a duty hereafter to hate his uncle. And to be even more supportive of poor Leonora. Who must never find out…

By the waterfront steps outside the Fat Lamprey one small insight remained to help unmake his day. What fool, he wondered, shipping the oars, had decided to call the dinghy *Heartsease*?

XVI

All my labours here by the river are done the better to blend this world's reality, as people are pleased to call it, with its enduring illusions. I have recently purchased a decrepit old punt, so that I may work almost at the waterline, with its splendid aspect hereabouts of a lofty row of poplars, trunks bare almost to the crown and twice their seeming height, at least for so long as their reflection stays untroubled, by the breeze, or by some wretched waterfowl leaving its wake. The closer one is to the water's surface, the more mesmerizing the effect, like an aviator lost between blue sea and sky, & confusing mysterious depths with airy infinity...

Letter of 3 July 1916 from Edith Hart to her brother Edwin

'Michael? Hello? Is something not all right?'

'Uh…who with?'

'With you, Michael, of course. What has happened?'

'What…? Er, which what has happened? What kind of what?'

Somehow Mike had dozed off on deck, post-breakfast – they were all sleeping longer each day – in a folding chair designed to make any creature loll. Even the sun on his face, alternating with shade as they chugged along, had done nothing to wake him. Unlike Bianca's phone call.

Consciousness advanced, to a moment headed, Oh, God!

'Oh God, I'm sorry – I didn't manage to call yesterday…'

'And now I am very anxious for you. We are all anxious, with you being all these hundreds of miles away from where I am, so that I am prevented from taking good care of you.'

Mike's mind might be unfocused, but Bianca's voice was as clear as if she stood silhouetted before him, with the sun blasting light hither and thence from behind her.

'I'm sorry, I forgot,' he pictured himself saying – just for one hyper-oxygenated moment of free-speech-though-the-heavens-come-tumbling-down.

What he really said was, 'Darling, I hope you can find it in your heart to forgive me. It's been a bit frantic here. The boat's engine got clogged up and Eliot had to dive down and clear it, and cut his knee on the propeller; and then for some reason we decided to have a foraged meal, and that turned out to disagree with the others; and then we had to pay a visit to Chris's aunt, who was in the neighbourhood … Oh, and poor Monty was sick …'

He'd been no such thing. But given some of what he sniffed out when being walked, Mike thought he bloody well deserved to be.

'Oh, no! Will he recover? ...Michael, are you sure?'

When at length he rang off, did his inner self bow its head in shame at the fact of My First Lie? Well, no actually. Maybe it was the prospect of yet more sun-smitten, purpose-free days of all-male snooze and booze. Or perhaps he was sustained in unexpected ways after the vow he'd made earlier, resolve stiffening by degrees as they'd driven downriver and away from Oxford. From now on, whatever assailed his marriage would serve only to strengthen it. It was a cause in which nothing would hinder him, not even being inventive with the facts, if that would make his wife happy.

The thought left him more liberated than he could have imagined. As Mike went below to change out of his pyjamas before lunch, Eliot glanced up at him, almost with a double take, and Chris peered round a door. It was, they both realized, the first time since God knew when, that they'd heard Mike whistling.

Something else was new.

'Designer stubble, is it?'

Until now Mike hadn't given it a thought.

'Nope,' he said. With a flourish he added, 'It's a beard!'

*

They'd all begun to slip, and go happily to seed. At a corner shop near their mooring back in Oxford, already Eliot, garnering a rucksack's worth of potential fry-up, had been steadily watched on a security screen. He was bound to make the owner inquisitive, with his uncombed hair and filthy deck shoes, every eyelet caked in mud. And right from the start of the *Speedwell*'s voyage he and Chris had supped without a thought on whatever they fancied: wild-boar-and-quince-sausage cassoulet, or Beaufortshire beef and ale pie plus an extra jug of gravy and hand-cut, triple-cooked chips. Mike, his body a temple or what, had kept to the likes of an undressed chicken salad, bulked out with such stuff as sugar snaps, asparagus, pomegranate, fennel or grapefruit, plus an indefinitely compressible hillock of rocket.

'You buggers can scoff in both senses if you want. See if I care.'

But as they idled – or idylled, so Chris said – towards the Chiltern Hills, no longer did Mike bother to laugh in the face of pudding and its manifold menace to health. One day's journey below Oxford, while the others demolished their sticky toffee pudding and grand Marnier soufflé, he'd embraced indiscipline enough to order a mango sorbet though please hold the raspberry coulis. Past Long Wittenham, at The World Turned All About, whose pub sign depicted its own watery reflection, his friends tactfully didn't notice a thing as he put his digestive system around a helping of apple and cinnamon tart with an added clotted-cream ice. What though last month his waist was mere enough for an Olympic swimmer? If it was okay bending the truth to keep Bianca happy when he forgot to phone, how could it be a sin against his marriage or himself to accrete the makings of a paunch?

Amid the creeping laxity of doodling down the river, on board the *Speedwell* the sense of time diminished.

Dates were being missed even though the cause of scholarship, policed by Eliot, still meant every Aunt-Edith-connected site got visited somehow. Already they'd missed a rock festival staged annually on water meadows below Abingdon by a famous and indestructible group still lean and lively after fifty years – even the drummer hadn't died. Over a late-night bottle of Calvados shared on deck in forgetfulness of how far unlowered voices carried over water, all sorts of plans were spoken of in vain. Much earnest resolve went towards seeing an open-air performance from the *Ludus Coventriae* Mystery Plays, being staged nearby at Wencaster-on-Thames. By the time the *Speedwell* ambled alongside her mooring for real, this show too had finished its brief run. Replacing the story arcs of Lucifer, Lazarus and Noah or whoever, was a carnival claiming to celebrate two thousand years of history during which Wencaster had been not just a town, but a seat of Saxon kingship complete with a wattle and thatch palace and the occasional parliament.

Anticipating the parade, Chris had looked forward to being entertained by the spectacle of bedsheet Romans, and medieval kings cloaked in cast-off curtains. But when fifty elaborate floats did pass down the High Street, what they offered was an animated Yellow Pages, mostly personified by teenage carnival queens enthroned amid flimsily garbed maids of honour. Miss Oxfordshire County Council led the procession; prominent too were Miss Swindon, and Miss Vale of Aylesbury Machine Tools…

The parade made its way to a grassy public space by the parish church, formerly part of a great abbey, together with the ruins of a once beautiful Lady Chapel. An enormous yew had grown up in front of the altar stone, laid on the site of a Dark Ages massacre, whose jumbled dead had doubtless fed the great tree's roots. Here, where not only the disintegrated slain but the battle itself was now known only to God and a few specialized history departments, there were candy-floss sellers and toy-rifle ranges, and a fancy-dress contest for the under-twelves, all tutus and plastic tiaras and shy little-girl pride. If only for the length of a shutter's click, an image of his daughter Jessie flashed upon Mike's memory. She once had that look in her face, with her soft small limbs dressed in a mass of yellow crepe paper as … yes, a buttercup …

It was the same at other sites. Weeks beforehand, Eliot had gone on line and logged the opening times of local museums, great houses and often-closed-up churches with a care that made even his own reading list look as unpretentious as a tabloid quiz. Not that he'd wanted to remind the others of his schedule, lest he made himself feel like an inconsiderate host.

'You're the captain,' Mike had said one evening. They'd been making their way back along the towpath from supper in rural darkness, when it became obvious they'd no idea where they were. Their guffaws could have woken people half a dozen moorings away. 'That means you tell us what to do. And we get to blame you for everything.'

So the itinerary remained, and Eliot still got to take his site photos and type up his notes. But his undeclared timetable was stuffed from the start.

For Chris there was just one date that had to be kept.

As a setting for Imogen's delayed birthday party Leonora, or rather her PA, the ever-present, semi-invisible Janet, had booked a coveted riverside venue. Jeeves had nothing on Janet, whom Chris suspected in this case of using her employer's name and connections to jump a lengthy queue. It was impossible to imagine her having a life of her own; in a moment's curiosity he'd said as much to the others.

'So,' Mike answered, 'where do you think she goes when she's not there being perfect?'

'Beamed up, of course. Off-planet, the same as all of them. The ones whose boss calls them totally loyal.'

The place appointed was a former Oxford college houseboat, nearly the last of its kind, all teak decks and carved woodwork painted white. It had been bought up by one of the rock stars whose gig they'd missed at Abingdon, and moored thirty miles downriver from its original site, by a half-acre eyot called Whim-Wham Island. The name commemorated a once fashionable pudding served there in a long-gone Doric temple to guests of the neighbouring country house, including one or two notoriously over-excited gatherings of the Hell-Fire Club. At a cost massively exceeding any new build, the boat had been converted to a recording studio, and was rented out for partying, so Leonora implied, as a very great favour indeed.

'It was rather expensive, you know,' she'd confided, when Chris had called to confirm that they'd be there.

Each day in the dinghy meanwhile, Chris heaved and strained like someone in labour, as if one more reach of the river would shrink and fade out any thought of his last encounter with Professor Wetherly.

'...Has your aunt explained her decision to transfer her daughter into the care of the NHS ... To be treated, after all, by people with less knowledge of her history...?'

'Have you ever thought that your aunt's – well, famously impulsive generosity, it must be said – was sometimes practised as, say, a plea for your cooperation in some way? For example in the form of hospitality, expenses met, or an unexpected gift ...?'

'Never. Absolutely not.' Chris's look had been as unyielding as a prison wall. 'Unless you count being a mother to me as some kind of bribe.'

'... And if, indeed, there could have been anything in your cousin's relations with her father that your aunt might consider, well, yes, inappropriate... how, in your opinion would your aunt have responded? If, for example, her daughter had appealed to her for support ...?'

At the time, Chris had been too full of unfocused fury even to concede the truth of Wetherly's analysis. He'd made his unthinkingly polite exit from the consulting room without any direct mention of his uncle's sly, brutish wrongdoing. Since then, as the river daily carried them further away, he began to call his rabble of angry emotions to some kind of order. Even in childhood he could sometimes prove himself one of nature's grown-ups; now raw feeling gradually found itself opposed by deliberate thought, and eventually by resolve. Grieve though he might for the once cherished memory of his uncle's cheerful fostering, it was selfish to mourn his own loss compared to the slaying of his cousin's innocence.

And a new burden of responsibility must be shouldered.

Leonora must be kept in ignorance. He tried to picture her response otherwise, and failed. Nothing suggested to him what she might do or say about her husband's multiple betrayal, either in character as her public persona or in deepest privacy. As if the dinghy were a fixed point and it was the river he laboured to move, Chris heaved on the oars more mightily than ever, and groaned aloud.

XVII

At the chosen moment [JohnWilkes] pulled [a] cord and out popped the wretched [baboon] which leaped onto the shoulders of Lord Sandwich, who ...concluded that the Devil had obeyed his summons in good earnest and had come to carry him bodily away. The harder he tried to shake off the poor creature the tighter it clung, whilst Sandwich cried out: 'Spare me gracious Devil: spare a wretch who never was sincerely your servant. I sinned only from vanity of being in the fashion; thou knowest I never have been half so wicked as I pretended: never have been able to commit the thousandth part of the vices which I have boasted of ... leave me therefore and go to those who are more truly devoted to your service ...I am but half a sinner.' ...

Describing a satanic ritual of The Hell-Fire Club at Medmenham Abbey near Henley, in *Chrysal, or the Adventure of a Guinea*, Charles Johnstone, 1760-65

On board the recording studio a huge bouquet formed a background to the seat of honour. A smaller version had been sent to Imogen on her birthday itself, following much deliberation between Martha and Chris and likewise in the language of flowers. Mostly it had featured lily of the valley – 'For a birthday at the end of May. Plus it signifies a return to happiness, the chart says here.' On the phone, Martha had sounded doubtful of her facts, if determined to give pleasure the best way they both could. For either of them, even decoding the Rosetta Stone would have been a preferred option.

Because it was now June, roses were also conspicuous in the lush, codified bouquet Martha had ordered.

'Red roses for love and appreciation,' she'd texted Chris. 'Or so my online sources say. Irises for friendship, faith, hope, wisdom, courage. Ivy for fidelity and respect. Just so you know.'

The language of flowers was repeated in festoons around the saloon where dinner would be served, and in the forget-me-nots and miniature irises of the table decorations. Looking around, Chris was reassured that no neglected detail could survive the discreet omnipresence of his aunt's PA. Infallible Janet was dressed as if to say, of course I'm polite enough to put on a party frock and a necklace for the occasion; but it would be inappropriate to stand out. As ever, she looked like an actress who might be naturally plain or who, alternatively, had put on homeliness as a professional tour de force. It was impossible to tell her age. Chronologically she might even be young.

Elaborately candlelit, the table settings for twenty

guests gleamed and glittered like a dragon's hoard; and seated at a baby grand a hired pianist was preparing to play the kind of music you noticed only if it stopped. Chris and the others were there early. They hadn't seen each other looking so sorted and clean since first casting off in the Cotswolds; this far downriver the effect was slightly unfamiliar.

When no one was watching, Chris sneaked a look at the engraved place cards.

'Who comes to your party,' he'd said to Martha, 'if you live banged up?'

'Leonora will think of something.' Martha had wanted to add, 'She does collect people, after all.' It was what Chris would have said himself. At least, if she hadn't been his foster-mother.

Sure enough, he recognized none of the names. Maybe they were from Leonora's working life? His unspoken suspicions came true when the guests started to arrive, and Janet, in a rare moment of confiding, said, 'Leonora thought Imogen would like to meet people of her own age. And I think your aunt was right to say that a lot of her own younger colleagues might feel honoured to be personally invited. To a family party like this.'

These were ambitious, presentable young people, probably living on parental handouts while their entire salary still went on parking the car. Even Chris understood his aunt enough to know that for junior staff her hospitality sometimes came at a price: manning the bar all night, or taking coats at the door. As it was they each circulated to fill the space well enough, starting at first on the ex-

houseboat's balustraded roof where champagne was being served. When Imogen arrived, looking almost like one of them in a low-cut party dress Chris hadn't seen before, any number of guests were ready to take pains and treat her, in mostly female twos and threes, like a long-established friend.

Eliot had only just got there before the other arrivals. On the *Speedwell* his departure had been delayed by an email from Marina.

'I thought I wouldn't bother you by phoning. But do please remember me to Chris's cousin on her birthday – you did say, the other day, that she was having a party. That is, I don't expect she'll remember me, but we did meet once, when she was quite little. Anyway … All my love. For what that's been worth to you …'

While Eliot typed what he hoped was the right response, he thanked the Celestial Historian whom he didn't believe in, that a long-ago law had banned skywriting, or any other large-scale public messaging that Marina might have contrived. He could see it even so: his name with added soppy stuff, up there in vivid loops of aircraft exhaust. And praise be that even if it was still legal she couldn't afford the hire of a small plane to fly up and down the Goring Gap hauling a personalised banner. 'Please, please, please think', one side read in his imagination; and on the other, 'of my lovable and loving son'.

The quaffing of Bollinger had gone on for a quarter hour longer than one might expect, when Janet raised a query. Already it was only an hour to sunset, with the wooded river cliff across the valley masked in shadow.

'Chris. Might I have a word?'

Was it Leonora? A second place of honour had been set for her; and she'd been due some time ago, to greet the guests as they arrived.

Janet looked as she usually did, simultaneously alert and untroubled. As if one could expect anything else of her.

'It's not like her to be late,' she confided. 'I thought – since you're here – would you mind being the one to call her? As a family member…?'

At the dark end of Whim-Wham island the music and chatter was distant enough for Chris to use his phone; but to no effect. For form's sake he left a message and briefly went on board to confirm that supper should be served. Back on the riverbank amid the expanding dusk with its splishing sounds from unidentifiable wild creatures, he tried various numbers including his aunt's home. On many an evening, however late, it had been Janet or some other staff member who'd answered the phone at her house. Leonora never considered herself at leisure, and scarcely distinguished between home and any other workplace. But for once the house by Primrose Hill was unpeopled; the phone just rang, not even inviting a message.

Chris returned to the party, to sit by Imogen and catch up, pretending not to gulp his venison pate and baby vegetables on fast forward. She seemed not to notice her mother's empty place at the opposite end of the table. At first this caused him an ache of dread; did it betoken indifference, or denial? Or another massive collapse of personality, all the way back to her worst times of blank withdrawal? Had too much been asked in putting her at the centre of this swirl of sociability?

He was about to get up again, by now imagining some accident to his aunt, whether freakish and grotesque or commonplace and dire. Beside him at that moment Imogen laughed: an ordinary laugh, shared with some of the people nearest her. An astonishing, almost unbelievable laugh. Chris realized he hadn't heard her do that for years.

As he got to his feet she turned to him. The remains of a smile glimmered.

'Oh, Chris, don't take too much trouble. Not if you're trying to call Mummy. If you were going to get her, you probably would've by now.'

Imogen acting sane? This was too confusing. He said something meant to be harmless and went out to call the newspaper for which Leonora worked. At no hour of the night or day were its headquarters quite empty; but this time all he got was advice to call numbers he'd just tried. When he returned, Eliot had taken Chris's place so that Imogen wasn't next to an empty chair, and the poached salmon with artichokes was being served.

At what point should he stop feeling frustrated, and let Leonora's uncharacteristic absence make him anxious instead? He'd just reached this stage of fretfulness when Janet appeared by his chair. For the first time ever she wore a small frown.

'I should have checked this sooner,' she said, when they were outside. She held out a phone. 'I have to keep several diaries for Leonora; but it's only on this one that she's moved a date without mentioning it. Look! ... Well, yes, it's an appointment she had with a health spa near Tetbury. Only, she said she had to transfer it at the last moment, to this weekend…All this is my fault. I really should have looked.'

'For God's sake, woman!,' Chris responded, more impatiently than he'd meant. 'This is her fault entirely.'

When in due course he reached the switchboard of Scotney's ('Let your stresses melt away in this magnificent destination spa') he was ready to be less forgivable than at any time in his life.

The receptionist's tone of glutinous deference made it worse.

'… I'm so sorry but Mrs Lovell isn't taking calls right now, I'm afraid.'

'From me she is.'

Leonora, guarded but gushing, was even more effusive than the receptionist. She knew she'd been terribly naughty and ought to say sorry.

Chris said, 'Well?'

'What is it, Crispin darling?'

He said nothing. Let her be the one to fill the silence. A low trick, but see if he cared.

'Darling, what's the matter?'

It wasn't going to help her, trying appeasement. He let another silence build, then said, 'What are you doing there? You owe several people an answer. What are you doing *there*?'

'Oh, Crispin! Darling boy. I know what you're thinking. Really I do.'

'Don't be so sure of that.'

'Oh, but I do. Please try to understand. You of all people will appreciate everything I've been through recently.'

Better than you know. At long last. Somehow he managed not to say the words out loud. Faced with his aunt's show of hostility to her own daughter, his anger made him numb. Leonora, innocent of Imogen's wrongs? He was ashamed that he'd ever thought such a thing.

Without hope of a serious reply he nevertheless demanded, 'Is there anything – at all – that I should pass on from you as a message?'

'Oh, darling, Janet will make people understand. If you'd rather not do it yourself. But I just needed this me-time so badly...'

Ringing off, two things astounded him. One: the restraint with which he'd just said goodbye, almost as polite as when leaving his other barely tolerable encounter that week, in Professor Wetherly's consulting room. Two: the furtive, stony purpose with which his aunt, at the gathering in Imogen's honour, had contrived her own non-appearance.

Immediately afterwards he called the same number.

Was there a waiting list at Scotney's for would-be guests?

'Unfortunately, sir, we are obliged to request that guests put their names down several weeks in advance.'

'Of course you are.'

There was one more surprise. As the party broke up, later than expected, Imogen had asked to cancel her taxi so that she could accept a lift from a young couple she'd got talking to at supper. On the way out she turned and thanked him.

'…For everything. And give my love to Martha and Tom.'

Just like a normal person. Chris found he had no idea what to make of her. She'd been down in the pit among demons for so long, there was no telling how her grown-up self, restored to health, would be supposed to look and sound. As it was, he felt as if the Imogen he'd known so long had been impersonated all evening by an actor. She was still militantly vegetarian, like the disorganised last time they'd eaten together, on board the *Speedwell*; she was also teetotal. So it was nothing but good cheer, additive-free, that must have given her that unfamiliar delicate flush.

'Oh, and Chris. Whatever Mummy's really said about why she wasn't here … Don't mind her. You're not used to it, and I am.'

Departing, she'd actually embraced him on her own initiative. This time it was his turn to be confused and dumb.

XVIII

Dear Islander,

...on the date given we are holding a Bank Holiday childrens' party and barbecue at the west end of the Island (two adults per mooring, plus children); prices per head as below. This being also the official birthday of Her Majesty the Queen, we would be grateful if you would decorate your boat, to help make this year's party a memorable one. We would also ask that residents seek to keep up their usual high standard in the matter of window-boxes, etc.

...and as this is a special occasion, outdoor chairs, tables, etc. will be permitted on the island, for the duration ...Likewise, registered moorers may sleep on boats overnight, provided permission is sought from the Committee in writing ...

Following the Island's last monthly meeting, the Committee would like to offer especial thanks to Mr Baines for his help. The Island's No Trespassers sign is once again as legible as any of us should wish it to be ...

Minutes of Pease Pudding Ait Committee

It was Whim-Wham Island with its aristocratic if sulphurous associations that had inspired the naming of Pease Pudding Ait, a lesser piece of ground half a mile downriver. Sir Francis Dashwood and his fellow satanists had by then passed far enough into history to be perceived as nothing naughtier than costumed figures in an historical tableau. The neighbourhood had long since changed, with the building of the railway. Within another generation the medieval manor house on the hillside above had been replaced with a vast pseudo-Florentine palazzo; and on account of this monstrosity trains called at the local station as if at a lodge gate, bringing flocks of servants and hillocks of luggage in the wake of weekend house guests. Unfamiliar foods were delivered to the kitchens of the new mansion; one train stopped just to unload a fresh pineapple.

A lifetime later a smaller, unpretentious settlement grew up on the damp little island nearby, till then ignored and anonymous. At one end of the newly named Pease Pottage Ait a prim assortment of bungalows, clapboard or prefab, stood on each side of a gravel path like the High Street in a model village. You could see why no one had bothered to build here before; in case of flood each Happy Valley and Place to Be was supported at the corners by a stumpy column of cheap lining bricks, like a car up on blocks.

The river was flooding now, though there'd been no rain for weeks. Even as Imogen's guests had partied under an opalescent, then star-strewn sky, the waters had been rising. Fifty miles away unseasonal thunderclouds had piled themselves, then douched the suddenly darkened Cotswold hills. This morning the *Speedwell* was straining at her tethers like a half-broken horse; and of Pease Pudding Ait – the island itself – there was no sign.

Of course every home still stood, just as it did through every winter's direst inundation. But the neat little gardens, like the island path itself, were under half a metre of rushing water; beneath the buildings a standing wave broke against each brick pillar like a bow wave, so that an intrepid, square-keeled fleet of bungalows appeared to be surging upriver. Raised verandas were piled with rescued garden furniture and the odd canoe; by one set of wooden front steps a garden gnome had the appearance of a displaced figurehead without a ship, as the waters swirled around his waist.

On board the *Speedwell* it felt worse moored against the bank than if they'd been carried away downriver, running before the flood. In the galley nothing seemed safe; already a teacup had fallen and smashed. But could they move on, or was Pease Pudding Lock impassable, with both gates of its chamber open to let the torrent surge through?

The new day, and its first crisis, had been announced by Monty. No one had heard him bark before, down below the deck. Surely he was better trained than that; far too much the canine gentleman. But there he was, sitting beside Eliot's bunk and woofing steadfastly at Mike. Louder, in that enclosed space, than a smoke alarm.

Eliot's case wasn't desperate; but Monty had a point. Enfeebled, and pale beneath a recent layer of sunburn,

Eliot was paying the price for an impulse he'd meant to indulge since they'd first embarked.

'Must have swallowed too much river,' he muttered without opening his eyes. He'd been swimming; and following a crisis dash for the lavatory at four in the morning it was evident that his insides were being vandalised by some species of vile bacterial squatter.

It had promised to be great, like all sorts of stuff you hope not to regret. Eliot was a strong swimmer, a fact he'd relished at many times and places in the course of business. Off Mykonos; or in the Coromandel Sea... Yesterday, minutes after sunrise with the riverscape holding its breath, the waters' shimmer had evoked the very essence of holy baptism. It occurred to him, as he'd leapt from the bows – being athletic wasn't always the same as elegance – that this was the nearest thing to immersion in the fountainhead of Edith's inspiration. Foremost in his imagination was the idea, got from her correspondence, of swimming in the river 'up an obliterating path of sunlight, as if in some otherworldly medium'. A broad bar of molten light did lie upon the face of the Isis, and he celebrated by sploshing about in it every way he could: diving like a dolphin, rolling front to back, floating triumphant with a sense of physical strength still unused.

But otherwise there wasn't much of a view from down at water level. You couldn't see a thing beyond a reedy margin and the stands of purple loosestrife along the banks. None of Edith's silvery pollard willows were in view, wandering in line along a ditch or rill as though anchored by their own damp azure shade. Whenever she'd painted a bright, misty light like this, statuesque elms and poplars were rendered as so many receding blue-grey profiles. For any swimmer though, they too were invisible. In any case, with so much water in his eyes it scarcely mattered what colours there were. His aunt had written of deep rose madder, burnt siena and emerald green; but as Eliot swam he might as well have been seeing in monochrome, like a soaked cat.

Twenty-four hours later, nauseous and prone, he recalled that for all he knew Edith never swam anywhere, even in the shallow end of a public bath. When her letters described the river laid with gules of golden light, she'd been writing to Stanley Spencer and quoting something he'd said. That bounder (Eliot had the historian's instinctive tendency to describe people in the language of their own time). Her wretched affair with him had been too brief to dignify with any such description as doomed. But it had left her heart not sore, so much as gouged and rent. Only now did Eliot find this coming back to him, as he lay amid twisted sheets with the feeling that he'd sweated out half the tainted Thames.

Monty was quieted, and offers of tea and dry toast refused as strenuously as the patient's feeble state allowed. Privacy seemed at a premium; also it would have been inhumane to fill the boat with breakfast smells of fried duck eggs and thick-cut gammon. So after a quick scoff of croissants and jam the others went ashore, to see if the river's altered state had marooned them.

'Trained for search and rescue, do you think?' Chris asked, as he and Mike walked down to the nearest lock. He indicated Monty, alert and straining on his lead.

'He could have been. Maybe explosives … My wife hasn't said.'

Any mention of Bianca, replacement spouse, still felt awkward within the easy habits of their friendship. The one time they'd all met, she'd listened with serious attention as well-worn daft catchphrases were explained, and cherished old jokes were mentioned then discreetly suppressed.

To avoid any pause, Chris asked, What latest news?

'Fine, fine. Everything's good. Well, there's a delay, in fact, before she can come home. About a week.' Mike mentioned some family detail back in Lisbon, a christening or something. 'Which is frustrating, of course.'

'Oh. Yes, indeed.'

Mike did feel genuinely thwarted by the delayed reappearance of his wife. It was all very well, yielding like this to the enforced freedom of the river. But being free was not real life. No one could properly define himself by getting a sunburned nose, and not caring if they all stayed up till the ghostly June dusk sidled round to the sunrise side of the sky. The measure of a man was in how he sized up to his responsibilities. Besides, the anticipation of their ultimate, proper marriage, in their own home, was now almost a rooted habit; putting it off had given his expectations, and his resolve, quite a jolt.

He said, 'We need a gnarled old lock-keeper. By the next bend in the river. Someone possessed of age-old wisdom, who'll tell us if we can sail on.'

The next bend produced the lock, just where the map had promised. There was also a lock-keeper. He was recently escaped from a career in teaching, with a pregnant wife and thirty years to go before anything resembling a gnarl. This lock was fine, he told them, and pulled a phone from his pocket to show the day's local changes to the river gradient. Within the lock chamber the fall between upper and lower sills would still be low enough to let them through.

'But then you might really be in trouble.'

With the river suddenly so high, Ham Bridge, a short distance below, had almost no clearance; it was impassable to anything bigger than a skiff. Or should he say, raising his voice above the unseasonal roar from the nearby weir, a skiff manned by a lunatic.

Thirty hours should see them back to normal.

They went to look at the bridge and sink a nominal pre-lunch beer in the Packhorse. Just about every crossing over the Thames has a pub at one end if it's old enough; Ham Bridge had met this qualifier since the Wars of the Roses. On the garden terrace they sat in a welcome patch of shade and watched the waves bearing broken leafy branches and other flotsam, amid explosions of light sparked from their surface by the unclouded sun.

Chris stretched out his legs and said, 'This is all very well. Being castaways -' gesturing with his pint '- like this. But Eliot'd better brace up soon. As long as he's languishing in a diseased state, we've got no Captain.'

'Fuck. No one to remember the important stuff. Drinking-water points. Refuse sites. Correct markings of cocks on fuel feed pipes.'

'Shit-stations. For pumping out. D'you know how to operate one of those?'

'Nope. Can't those pumps blow back at you?'

'That's what the barman said the other night.'

'Eh?'

'In the Haywain. Just this side of Oxford.'

'The which?'

'In Silicone Gulch. Full of professional geeks. You complained how young they all were.'

'Oh, yeah. Ancient boozer. Like an old-fashioned shape of haystack, only with roses up it and windows.'

They paused and sipped.

'And do you know the navigation symbols? Colour-coded spheres and cones, for things like shoals and wrecks?'

'Uh … You?'

'Nope.'

'But at least that's stuff you know you don't know.'

'Of course Eliot always was going to run a, um –'

'- Yeah, tight ship.'

'Be doing violence to his own nature, otherwise.'

'Do you know, we're even insured against sonic boom?'

'And why not? I'll drink to that.'

'Yeah, it's his boat…Me too …'

XIX

Those attending the Regatta ... must dress in accordance with long-established tradition.

Gentlemen are required to wear lounge suits, or jackets or blazers with flannels; and a tie or cravat.

Ladies are required to wear dresses or skirts with a hemline below the knee and will not be admitted wearing divided skirts, culottes or trousers of any kind...

Whilst not a requirement it is customary for ladies to wear hats.

From a Regatta Etiquette Guide, middle Thames valley,
early twenty-first century

Many towns on the River Thames stand back from the waterfront. Sometimes they're almost hidden, as you sail on past flat meadows or public parkland. A large old bridge slides into view, with massy balustrades, or stone niches built to shelter foot-travellers from any packhorses or passing carts. Stay on the boat, and once you've passed it you're back in empty flood-prone countryside, as if you've sailed past nothing more than a folly spanning an artificial lake below some country house. But should you disembark and climb the steps onto the roadway, chances are you'll be instantly at the meeting of several busy streets; in a broad market square perhaps, or looking up at a beautiful Renaissance town hall, from when this place was once the county's seat of government.

'If I were Marquis of a place like Reading,' Chris said next day over a map depicting several square miles of banal exurbia, 'I'd apply for demotion.'

Yet as he spoke, even Reading was making a show of its own invisibility. With Eliot back at the wheel, briefly several pounds lighter, the *Speedwell* made its way between wooded river cliffs and flat sports fields, and past the only ground high enough for the town's bridge and its resounding traffic. As they sailed past thickets of reeds and willow and acres of mown grass, the noise of the town centre seemed piped from some vast sound system; on the main-line station's PA, every word was audible. Meanwhile the town could only be glimpsed, set back from the river beyond a foreground of trees. In the morning light an array of massive glass towers, tall shining ghosts, made a procession across the bottom of the sky.

The nearness of a large settlement brought waterborne suburbs. Beyond a narrow cut a huge marina lay unseen; and for several miles between insect-brimming hayfields there extended a ribbon development of houseboats. With the eye of a professional tour operator, Eliot noted no towpath and wondered how far to the shops. Mike too, whether or not thinking of his own muddy gaff in tidal Twickenham, eyed the line-up of pastoral idylls, and pictured grinding treks beneath a rucksack freighted with tinned food.

At Henley they had to tie up some way above the town. It was Regatta Week and moorings were hard to find. The town bridge for once was dense with pedestrians rather than vehicles. The gargoyles on the tall flint tower of St Mary the Virgin would be surprised could they see the alteration below them each year. For centuries they'd been beaten about by the elements, or borne the weight of icicles and snow or jackdaw guano of late-medieval, even Early English date. Cracked and eroded they might be, and sometimes tactlessly replaced. But for much of their history the scene beneath had been never-changing. Only during the Regatta did such crowds surge across the river. Whereas the Thames ran smooth and dignified, the stream of people above, sporting the fanciful boating titfers of both sexes, resembled a shallow brook strewn with every hue of confetti.

Marina was there, as every year. She'd arrived on a stopping train from Paddington, changing at Twyford where three hundred passengers had alighted to separate themselves from the rest of humankind and await the Henley connection. With the platform to themselves they'd resembled a regatta-bound Gilbert and Sullivan chorus. Among the blazers and flimsy designer dresses, the only person who'd looked different was a young black woman, a high-viz-jacketed station employee. Her straightened hair was dyed purple, tied in a pony-tail and shaven at the sides in an elaborate pattern unmatched by any other barnet there. As the Henley train pulled in she was explaining the timetable to a woman in a strapless full-length dress, with expensively piled fair hair and a many-stranded pearl choker, who spoke English as a second language.

Such was the idiom shared by the human tributary that now flowed down the street from the small railway terminus at Henley. The train had had less standing room than the Tube at rush hour. But Marina's heart lifted as she approached the thronging waterfront. Here at last was proximity to the world of ticketed entrances and Members' champagne bars where she knew that, given the chance, she truly could belong.

She was dressed according to the strictures of the Stewards' Enclosure, sited within a high canvas wall near the Finishing Line. Marina had once actually penetrated this piece of ground, long ago as a junior species of Embassy wife. Since then, social instinct still made her cleave to its demands. She'd once experienced a defining moment in her sartorial awareness here at Henley, on seeing a female guest expelled from the Enclosure, with adamantine politeness, for observing only the spirit rather than the letter of the occasion. The luckless woman should have been a sight to please anyone, in her wide-brimmed straw hat and infinitely becoming halter top – but nothing, it seemed, could excuse her long, full-bottomed palazzo pants. Today Marina was discreetly garbed in a tight-waisted cream linen suit, with a small egret-feathered fascinator, and leather mules for not sinking too far into all the mud. She made the neatest contrast with one jolly group, made up of long-haired girls partying in balloon-skirted mini-dresses and gumboots caked with filth.

Without fail each summer Leonora also pitched up here. Not for her though, thirteen stops in standard class, and all the way no offer of a seat. With a couple of people she knew from the Chelsea Arts Council she'd travelled down in a black cab; later she planned to leave with others of the same party in their helicopter, from a field set aside for such things up beyond the Starters' Enclosure.

Chris had known to expect his aunt, having been texted with a time and place where they might meet.

'I hope you approve, Crispin darling,' she said. She'd booked them a waterfront café table, on a Members' Only stretch of riverbank near the bridge, where most of the cheering went on. 'I did have to reserve it a long time in advance. You have to, you know, if it's the Royal Enclosure.' Certainly nothing here could be further from the innocent soiled-bunting festivities, all chumminess and mucking in, on Pease Pudding Ait.

Now that he understood her, Chris could guess what was supposed to happen. Strawberries and cream must be consumed, and Buck's fizz tippled. Only then could the talk move on; till then it would be kept as innocent of discord as a comic-operatic overture.

Eventually Leonora dabbed the corners of her mouth, put down her napkin, and assumed a look of bottomless sincerity.

'I do appreciate that our last conversation may have seemed incomplete. Given the circumstances, we simply didn't have time to talk properly. Crispin dear, I do know that. I hope you understand.'

Since the calculated fiasco of Leonora's non-appearance at her daughter's birthday party, Chris had had no idea how today's meeting might go. But now that they were here, in this elaborately costumed crowd scene of meeting and greeting against distant band music – well, it was obvious. After all, when had he ever seen his aunt in back-off mode, never mind apologising? She meant to justify herself.

Yet that in itself betrayed her.

Chris had come resolved to pass for peaceable, no matter what would really be said. He enquired, pleasantly enough, 'How was Imogen, when you last saw her?'

'Very well, thank you. For her.' Watching him.

Most people only knew Chris as a decent man who expressed himself straightforwardly. It would shock them were they to see him, as now, turning bland and neutral towards someone he disrespected.

Since he'd spoken with her on the night of the birthday party, there'd remained one last hateful doubt.

'How often,' Professor Wetherly had demanded, 'would you say your aunt expresses sympathy for Imogen's condition?'

'Well, if you've heard her on radio or TV ...' Chris had known, really, that Leonora's public persona had nothing to do with it.

'Has her attitude to her daughter undergone any change? Say, in recent years?'

Yes, was the obvious reply. Unable to speak, Chris had

gestured to that effect…Since Imogen went mad: that was when. But surely it could have been coincidence? He'd gone on thinking so, right up to the disrupted celebration on the island.

Now, amid the self-conscious privilege of the Royal Enclosure, the obligation on a guest to say the right thing sat heavy on him, just as his aunt intended. Nonetheless he looked her in the eye and remarked, 'I suppose she'd been looking forward to her birthday party.' Wetherly, in his consulting room, could not have spoken more politely.

If Leonora had been an average sort of woman, she would have blushed. As it was, she exclaimed, 'Oh, Crispin darling, you know I normally ask after the girl more often than that.' She paused to smile at a passing grey-haired couple: the wife dressed as for a wedding, the husband in a blazer and tie whose coded significance one was doubtless meant to appreciate. 'Look,' she went on, 'I know you were angry when last we spoke. You had a right to be, and I respect you for it.'

'And …?' he managed not to say.

Straight-backed as ever, she returned his steady look. 'So I hope we understand each other better now. I was at fault to let you stay angry afterwards, and I apologise for that. I'm very sorry for that, Crispin; truly I am.'

He made a point of saying nothing, and she felt forced to add, 'Which is why I really want to emphasize how very much I hope this will draw a line under things. For us both…'

On the river, a race was surging to its climax; a wall of sound bore down on them as the cheering grew closer.

Briefly it grew hard to hear what she said. But gestures and expression alone were enough. While Leonora was inaudible, doubt could be seen to lurk behind her very self-control.

They waited till the shouting, far and near, had died away. He said, 'I found Professor Wetherly very direct in his questioning. In fact I don't think he avoided any aspect of Imogen's family relationships.' He paused. She stared at him as though nothing else existed. 'I take it he was equally frank with you.'

A less intelligent woman would have feigned bewilderment; then disbelief; then deep hurt. Seeing her turn pinched and pale, he had to pity her. But not at the cost of any compassion due to his cousin. There had even been a perverse sense of liberation in facing the dark truth of Imogen's recent life. In knowing at last what he ought to think, and what he had to do hereafter, to guard and champion her.

Meanwhile Leonora had muttered an excuse, and walked swiftly away.

X X

Say, Muse, shall Wee not quit the Towne,

Where Dunghill Steps and Pudding Lane in London's Ordures drowne

Beneath dead Dogges, flayed Sheepes' Heads and Hogges' Guts,

The waterborne Effluvia of foul Humanitee,

To where the chrystall Themmes doth yet run free

Where nymphs disport themselves and swains are gay

Among thy groves and pastures, sylvan Henley?...

'Thamesis Sordidus Redivivus', Will Fowler,
'the Bargee Poet' (1601-62)

Marina had also been lunching at Henley, as the guest of two former neighbours. She'd known the Gaskin-Jobbinses from the old days, when she'd been married to Roland's father and lived near Reigate in a mock-Tudor house with a half-acre garden, called The Dingle. Later that month she and Maud would get together again and they'd do the Chelsea Show, courtesy of the local flower-arranging society. For Marina there was no Members' Enclosure, but she and Maud and Donald made a suitable tableau in one of the grassy car parks, with their own canvas-roofed gazebo plus other signifiers of carefree leisure including linen napery, proper cutlery, and a heavy terracotta pot in which grew fresh mint for the Pimms.

As usual the Gaskin-Jobbinses had asked after Roland, whom they remembered as a small boy. But for once Marina had not bloomed into animation at her offspring's name; instead she'd hedged, and ventured a smile dimmed to fond indulgence. She didn't let on that in all likelihood Roly was somewhere here, much less betray how she pictured him. In her mind's eye he stood at the centre of a tableau rather different from their own, one that told a cautionary tale much in the High Victorian style of Frith's *Derby Day*.

Poor Marina knew little of the world into which her boy seemed to have strayed; in her version of it the figures surrounding him might just as well have materialized unchanged from the nineteenth century, in soiled top hats or suspiciously gaudy crinolines of cheap fabrics, aniline-dyed with draggled muddy hems. Behind him gaped the dark entrance to the tent where people went and placed their bets on the races, from which a man with a mean, too-intelligent face – so Marina would have put it – was emerging with his winnings. A young couple with a baby stood nearby, she sorrowing at their sudden loss, he shocked rigid. Accompanying Roland were a couple of men too repulsive to be called seducers, though that was how Marina would have styled them, each peering with feigned casualness into her darling's opened wallet. And of course there was a Woman, for Marina spared herself no angry apprehension concerning that son of hers.

At that instant indeed, in the real world some such person or persons were provoking a similar righteous fret in Monty, tied up to guard the boat. But whereas Marina, over lunch, was feigning sociable good cheer, Monty had no intention of wagging his tail and keeping his voice well modulated. Two of his three humans had just gone ashore into the Regatta's mile-long churning floor show. So only Mike had been on board, showering, when Monty exploded in a barrage of woofs.

Mike hadn't chosen to own a dog. Some sort of bond had grown between them nonetheless, if only as their household's only males. But overhearing Monty now, he scarcely knew him. By the time he'd got a towel round his waist and gone on deck, however, there was nothing left to see.

*

Espying Marina in that afternoon's crowds, Eliot was not dismayed, just braced. She'd said she would be here. He and Chris might normally have been downing a swift fortifier, standing as they were on the top deck of a Routemaster bus converted to a bar. But Chris was yet to have his encounter nearby with Leonora; so he too was mindful of a fraught exchange to come. It had to be strong coffee, squared shoulders, and each man's wits on inspection parade.

Marina had encountered them as Chris was disappearing into the Royal Enclosure to join his aunt.

'Are you going in there too?' she asked Eliot. Whatever else was on her mind, her social antennae still quivered at the sight of an acquaintance entering Elysium. Eliot recalled an art appreciation course she'd done – to keep up, in her Embassy days? – and had a momentary vision of the Enclosure as depicted on a grand classical ceiling. In place of kings and antique gods, accredited Members in straw trilbys, with their wives, glanced down from the edge of a thundercloud.

He gestured, no.

'You said you might like us to get together.' No reason to prevaricate. 'To talk about something?'

Her response was not what he expected. She gave a centre-stage start, as though he were the supplicant, and she the one surprised and casting about for an escape.

'Well, yes, of course. I mean, of course I did. I mean, just as soon as you all get to London – yes, I'd love to. But you know I do appreciate that you're on holiday, obviously. Shall we leave all that until later? I'm sure that's what you'd prefer.'

The poor woman was trying to look at him directly, but without success, as if the sun had got in her eyes. All around them the festive crowd ambled and surged; to Marina, intent on him, they might as well be ghosts.

'Sure. But if it's Roland and his prospects you want to talk about, isn't he here himself? I thought Chris said –'

'Oh, no!' For whatever reason, her mouth fell open in a gape of panic. For the first time since they were both young, he couldn't tell what she'd say next.

'No – no, he can't be. I mean, surely that must have been a mistake – whatever it was that Chris might have said; I'm sure it must. I know you'll be perfectly happy to wait until you're back in London … Won't you?'

Familiar as he was with Marina in self-defeat mode, Eliot's curiosity was pricked on by this sudden turnaround. So too was his largely humane desire to make her less clinging and unquiet. Sometime soon he figured he'd have to meet the boy Roland anyway, and get into character as a potential employer.

He said, 'Now that we're closer to town, perhaps he and I could meet somewhere en route.'

Marina's hunted look intensified. 'Would you mind – ' she breathed, looking up and lasering him with sincerity ' – Eliot, would you mind – would you forgive me – would it be really, really all right with you if I – if we – took just a teeny rain check on this? If I can contact Roly for you, he absolutely will be in touch with you. Right away – cross my heart. Promise me that would be all right. Won't it?'

From the range of masks he wore for her, this time only bland reassurance would do. Seeing her so troubled, he was even moved to ask if she'd like a cup of tea or something.

'Oh, no! No, really! That is so sweet of you, Eliot. But no, I couldn't – I won't. Besides, Maud and Donald will be waiting for me – at least,' with a show of looking at her watch – 'I'm sure they must be soon.' Half recovered now their meeting was over, as they parted she was almost coquettish. 'Look!' she exclaimed, 'I'm gone already.'

*

With hindsight Mike wondered if someone really had meant to sneak on board. Monty's next outburst, a few minutes later, was less impassioned, but only just. This time he did glimpse someone: youngish, dressed expensive-casual, with a haircut to command respect from the best barber in town. It was the same three-quarter rear view Chris thought he'd seen last night, in a swelling, raucous crowd drinking outside a pub in Bridge Street. As the man walked away, rapidly though with a limp, it wasn't wasted on Mike that he'd turned to glance back at the boat.

On active service and elsewhere, Mike had met enough sorts and conditions of men to read most of what he might see. Unlike Chris, he'd no reason to recognize the grown-up Roland. But he knew, instinctive as Monty detecting a faint but compromising scent, that this one was iffy. Many people, seeing a man with bruising and an uneven walk, might just figure him for a cyclist who'd been knocked down and had a miracle escape.

Mike sensed otherwise. Before leaving the *Speedwell* he took care to lower the blinds, and left poor Monty behind after all. If need be, to quiver to the tip of his rigid tail, and strain every muscle of his hairy canine person in barking himself hoarse.

XXI

In its suave defunctionalizing dissolution between the fabricated and the natural world, Netherbourne Mill House stands as one of the canonical works of the late twentieth century. The masculinity of its governing frame references the site's former purpose, whereas the interior's sensitively modulated interplay of transient light and mobile shade interposes an organicism that is entirely sui generis. In its controlled simplicity, its confident massing and the specific historical references of its handling, this work is unambiguously seminal...

Chris knew the guy who'd written this; liked him, even. He was a colleague, who in the bar of the Senior Common Room thankfully didn't sound one bit as if his working life was spent churning out such stuff.

Of course no one who wrote about the house could bang on about its far-reaching vocabulary of form or the poise and convergence of its governing ideas without describing the marvels of its site. A little Chiltern stream ran through the atrium, for God's sake, shooting sparks of light from beneath a floor of glass bricks. In its setting of woodland and water, few could see the place without an involuntary moment of pleasure; certainly not Chris, biking up through the cool shade of Park End Shaw at the end of a ten miles' journey away from the river.

What counted most for him was its place in his childhood. Never go back, they say; and on every return he'd expected the house, the reflecting millpond and the grand amphitheatre of trees to look smaller and somehow prosaic. What surprised him each time was how every familiar detail still kept the brightened high definition of boyhood.

The lane made a last turn towards the house and the half-hidden cottages beyond. Up here the Thames valley was just visible through a gap in the trees, as if seen through the wrong end of a telescope. In Chris's boyhood imagination it had been Netherbourne Pond, behind its high mossy dam, which almost supplanted the river as Ratty and Mole's entire universe.

The place hadn't even lost its innocence for him through all the times the family had been photographed here for articles about Leonora or once or twice filmed for TV. Irrationally, since his uncle's death he'd found himself thinking, How strange, never to see such a familiar place again – to start with surprise, almost, as he remembered, Hang on, I own it now! Going inside, as he made his way over floors of polished flagstone, cedar and oak, he felt like a time traveller, trying not to disturb all their earlier selves: the charismatic uncle and famous aunt, of whom he knew nothing but good; little Imogen, blithely chirruping; his own younger self.

He found one of them now, albeit slightly foxed. Leonora was in the living room, bending and stooping over an array of open cardboard boxes. Through the sliding glass wall leading to the sun deck, light reflecting from the pond reduced her almost to a silhouette.

Chris had expected her. He would have paid the house a visit anyway; but she had left a message asking if she could come and see him here.

'Now that this is your house – and rightly so – I wanted to take away everything of mine for you.

Said with dignity, of course. When Leonora wanted something, who knew what she'd suffer rather than blow it and be ingratiating?

She added, 'I do need your help though. So many of these things belong to you more than anyone else. Some of them from when you were quite a young boy. But I don't want to make any mistake, and interfere. It's so hard to know which are the objects people treasure from those early years. You came to us with some wonderful toys; yet what you cared for most was that old serving spoon you'd bought in a junk shop. It wasn't even real silver.'

Chris responded warily with something appreciative. He'd come prepared to wait while each of them edged towards what they really wanted to say. Also, since the rush of revelation about his adoptive family, for the first time since his teens he had the feeling of being caught completely off balance. Back in Class IIIA, realising his friend Milsom was merely extrovert rather than witty, with a sense of entitlement in place of real intelligence, Chris had astonished himself, as well as the other boy, by his own scathing hostility. He felt the same now, seeing Leonora pretending not to be afraid of him, and resolved to spare her what he could.

'Shall we go into the garden?' she said – and immediately apologised. 'I'm so sorry. I'd forgotten it's not my place to say that now.'

He suspected she was all too conscious of it, but gave a faint smile and said, no, he was the one who'd forgotten he was the new owner of the Mill House.

'No, but really,' she said, 'I hope it didn't look as though I was inviting myself up here,' gesturing around the beautiful home that had been such a feature of her well-publicized family life. Leonora's career had been strong on personal history. Witness the documentary she'd sent Chris's iPad: 'Ever since I learned to read my favourite childrens' books at my mother's knee, I was resolved to be as wonderful a wife and mother as she was...'

The background provided by her home life must have been a script that wrote itself, once Leonora started down this route to professional self-advertisement. Netherbourne may not have been as famous as the Old Parsonage at Grantchester, nor Dickens' home at Gad's Hill. But hell, nowhere could've photographed better. It certainly upstaged their real main home, in a Regency villa near Primrose Hill.

He and his aunt went out to sit above the closely tended wild-flower meadow by the pond; here, too, felt like stepping into an old photo of their former lives. No wonder this was where she'd wanted to meet him.

'I hope it's not too much of an imposition, coming all this way.' Leonora sounded like a queenly hostess to a valued acquaintance, rather than a foster-mother with one of her nearest. Hiding her anxiety at what he might say or do.

She added, 'We've had so little chance to talk recently. About so many things. Properly, away from the rest of the world.'

He agreed that there was a lot of catching up to do. Chris found he couldn't look her in the eye, so strong was his regret for times gone by. He stared at the dragonflies swerving over the ruffled water, the meadow flowering with rock roses and speedwell, wild thyme and rampion, like a scene in a pre-Raphaelite painting. Leonora gazed at him as steadily as at anyone in her public life of dispensing reassurance to others. They say intensity of attention can signify either great love or all-devouring hate. Neither was true of Leonora; but she'd always valued Chris's goodwill. He was after all the son she'd never borne

'You're married too,' she said. 'So you must understand some of what I've felt since losing my husband of so many years. By that, what I mean is years of bad and good things alike. So many experiences within marriage can prove an unbreakable bond, whatever they may seem to an outsider.

'And I did love him; even at moments when I didn't like him one bit. I think it only right to tell you that there were such times.'

' – I'm sure there were –'

'But it's the good times that endure, so long as one

survivor lives on to remember them. I wasn't always certain of that, however many heartfelt confidences I've been privileged to hear in my working life. But now I know – I truly know – that they're what will always remain of the marriage when every other part of it is taken away.'

It was as close as she could bring herself to pleading for his silence. But at least they might understand each other. She would talk with becoming discretion around the real cause of Imogen losing her mind; and he in turn would sit there being tactful. Polite. Considerate of others' feelings.

…Humane…

Or, a mealy-mouthed pillock, according to the mutterings of his good angel. His better self.

But Chris too had an agenda. In a neutral voice he asked, 'And how has Imogen responded, would you say? To her father's death.'

How many months, since Leonora last saw her daughter? It shocked him that he hadn't asked before.

'Don't you agree that she may be improving? Seeing how she looks now? You must have noticed too.'

His irony showed no effect. 'Oh, Crispin,' she sighed, 'who can really say? In such a case as this.'

Chris let a silence develop. He was damned if he wouldn't try to make her admit responsibility for her own daughter.

She said, 'Please understand. It's so important not to be misled by false hopes – by any change we might think there's been in that girl's condition.'

Chris noticed – how belatedly – the way 'this boy' had

always meant him affectionately, as in 'this boy of our very own' whereas 'this girl' had been a way of not mentioning Imogen by name.

He said, 'I haven't just seen her. I talked to Wetherly as well.'

'Yes. You know, you did tell me that.' This, in a voice meant to soften him.

'He seemed to think her chances of improvement were good.'

'But he's only one man!' Out of character for a moment, Leonora squeaked in protest. Collecting herself she said, 'Other excellent people have had care of her too.'

Yes, he wanted to say, who owed their careers to Imogen's father.

'And haven't you thought so as well?' he demanded. 'Whenever you must have seen her last. Or spoken to her, perhaps? … I suppose Imogen doesn't contact you by email?' Thinking, Like she's just asked if she can do with Martha and me.

'No, of course she doesn't!' Leonora was never snappish. Except unconsciously, when talking about her daughter. Another thing he'd missed; yet again he'd let himself be blindsided.

She added, 'That girl just wouldn't apply herself enough to do something like that.'

For his own sake as much as anything, he wanted to wrest just one straightforward answer from her. This was the woman, after all, who'd spared nothing to be a mother to him through the rawest years of his life, at an age when any injury to the feelings of the heart can pass on permanent harm to the soul itself. He pushed the thought away and persisted.

'But what was your own impression? The last times you've had contact.'

'Oh, please, Crispin darling. Which of us can really tell what we're trying to confront, in living with something like this? I'm really not a qualified person to judge, whatever the world may say.'

He wanted to shake her; stare her down; speak with the frankness she'd always said she prized in close relationships. But he knew she'd just slide aside, with modest self-deprecation maybe, or a show of ignorance: 'What dark betrayals, Crispin? Of whom? You say I've contributed? To what? I don't understand you ...' The more brutish and truthful she forced him to be, the more she'd defend herself with a righteous assault of her own: 'This is unthinkable. It's as though we've lived all these years with a stranger as one of our family...'

Forget it. He'd just have to work with the facts she was prepared to acknowledge.

'Under the terms of – of the will' – at that moment Chris couldn't face mentioning his uncle by name – 'I too am one of the people responsible for Imogen's welfare.' He couldn't miss how pompous he sounded. But so what? 'I won't presume to guess exactly what you do think about your daughter's condition.' He stared at Leonora, daring her to interrupt. 'But I'm duty bound to anticipate any and every likely outcome. Including a complete recovery.'

She stirred in her chair; but dared not protest. He went on to describe such possibilities in detail: altered regimes of treatment; in due course a transfer to the hospital's halfway house; more spending money; Imogen maybe coming to live with him and Martha.

She made a show of hearing him out; but only to buy time. His cousin might never regain her wits – had he thought about that? And how in conscience could they torment Imogen, as well as themselves, with false hopes of improvement? As for money, what use did she have for that?

'And the gamble of you both taking her into your own home! What about the possible effect on Tom – on your and Martha's son?'

To all this he managed to show no more response than when, say, he heard a first-year student describing Pol Pot as a man of vision, or Margaret Thatcher as the nation's greatest prime minister excepting only Winston Churchill. When she'd finished he allowed a pause, then said, 'There is one thing I've promised to do. When I last saw Imogen, she was emphatic about wanting to be at her father's memorial service.'

Could this be the first time Leonora's poise and fluency had failed completely? Gone AWOL? Left her utterly stuffed? Before she could stage a recovery he added, 'I think such a request has to be honoured. She's been especially concerned to hear the speech I'm composing for you – I mean, writing on her father's account.'

Leonora was speechless. Her foremost thought was that if some awful misunderstanding ever made someone like that girl into a holy saint, her emblem would surely be a loose cannon.

'The eulogy,' he persisted. 'Which I haven't quite finished writing.'

She murmured something about the heat out here. Yes, he said, do let's move inside.

Was this it, then? Would it always be like this? On both sides, polite evasion. While he, an honest man by nature as well as in principle, feigned honour to his elders by fibbing his head off. All the while – 'for everyone's sake, Crispin darling' – supping with a short spoon? In his mind's ear he heard his son Tom, innocent and free, taking the piss. 'Look at you. Standing in bullshit up to your eyelashes... Dad, TSD ...Yeah, Doctor of Taurean Scatology, or what?'

Before he left, Leonora asked if he'd like to look around the house. 'Your house, I mean. For old times' sake. While it's still how it used to be.'

He suppressed a shudder. 'That's really thoughtful of you. But no. Far too many ghosts.'

'I hope that won't always make it hard for you, Crispin dear. I mean, when you come to live here.'

It would, so he wouldn't. 'I'd rather remember everything just as it was. I'm letting the house. And putting the income into a fund for Imogen.' They were outside, by the mill stream. Bending to pick up his bike, he couldn't resist adding, 'Seeing that she's been left nothing.'

Somewhere above them a chiff-chaff sang, repetitive and blithe. A pigeon was cooing of summer and deep cool boscage, up in the unseen reaches of Great Wood, where lady's slipper orchids and the even rarer maiden's tresses hellebore, frail and spectral, were said to flower. As Chris was about to leave, Leonora couldn't stop herself saying,

'I'm so glad you were a happy little – littlish – boy here. That was partly why I insisted to my husband – to your uncle Hugh – that you should be the one to have this place for your own – to inherit the Mill House. It was my idea, you know. As a gift to you from both of us.'

'I'm sure it was.' He leaned to kiss her on the cheek, to hide his face in case it showed anything but astonished gratitude. 'No gift could have been more magnificent.'

She couldn't let him go without one last, heroically casual question.

'Oh – and tell me: how *is* the eulogy going?'

'Rather well, in fact. I wasn't sure how to start; but now it's going splendidly. I certainly think Imogen approves... Goodbye.'

He turned to freewheel down through the trees, liberated as a kestrel newly unhooded and cast into a vast bright sky.

XXII

7 hot pheasant and one for the king

6 quails for the king, partridge . . .

Chickens, artichoke pye, curlew roast, pease buttered, rabbits, ducks, plovers, red deer pie, pigs' ears soused, hot herons roast, gammons of bacon, made dish (thought to be a ragout), pear tart, palates of grease, dried tongue, turkey pie, pheasant pie, hog's cheek dried, turkey chicks cold

From a dinner menu for James I, August 1617

At breakfast on deck next day there was a sense of well-being. Chris had finished his speech; and Eliot had figured all he needed to concerning the boy Roland. Even Mike, cheerfully unkempt – 'You're not dishabille,' Chris said, 'you're a bum' – occasionally failed to dwell on his new marriage as a self-imposed project. For hours at a time he forgot to dwell on it at all.

Being on holiday usually took hold in the end, so Eliot pointed out. What his clients tended to do first was break out in minor ailments, from the shock of being at leisure. A week later came recovery and the start of sun- or windburn; and by the last four or five days of marine archaeology or walking an ancient pilgrimage route, unaccustomed ease and good humour prevailed.

It was in this last state of mind that the next evening was decided on as Blow-Out Night. There was no shortage hereabouts of high-end provender; so close to London, on fine days the landscape was convulsed with the quest for almost every kind of well-funded leisure. Waking late that morning, up through successive currents of confusion and stupor, at first Chris feared a flashback hallucination. What but a vast illusionary roc could be making those asthmatic noises on the cabin roof? Perched there with a view to carrying them off, boat and all. Expanding consciousness, then a contorted squint through the porthole, explained everything. What he'd heard was the heavy breathing of a passenger balloon being injected with extra helium to lift it over Ashendon Hill.

Recalling his dope-disordered moments under Oxford's non-existent elms, he was braced nonetheless to find the river paved over by Victorian day-trippers in punts, canoes and smoking-devil steam launches; the men in boaters and white flannels, the women corseted and bustled, under hats elaborate enough for table decorations. His apprehensions soon dissolved; the scene was entirely modern, with the air as crowded as the water. Hang gliders floated, high enough to cast a shadow no bigger than a buzzard's; and the valley was briefly noise-polluted by a local hobby-farmer taking his Cessna up for a spin. On the river, boats throbbed and the waters churned.

It was agreed that the holiday's outstanding night of excess should take place near Cookham at the Golden Pickerel, this being the nearest foodie shrine that didn't demand your name put down for a table at puberty. A century ago it had been the humble Maybush, a waterfront alehouse with sawdust on the floor and no food on sale that didn't announce 'tradition' as meaning no choice and few materials. These days its famously expensive menu made much of the T-word. In place of a pickled egg and a corned-beef sandwich on white bread made up as a favour, today's Michelin-starred owner had left no history of local foodstuffs unransacked. Round here, it seemed, no one's farm-labouring ancestors could have gone hungry, much less risked transportation for nicking a brace of coneys.

Out of respect for this menu the *Speedwell*'s crew had gone more or less unfed for a day. As they sat down to table their innards grumbled like a wind ensemble playing an overture, with the bassoons in a particularly low register. Whether from keen-edged appetite, or curiosity about what they were eating, near-silence ruled as they fell upon the starter: brain soufflé and roast fennel, comfrey-leaf fritters, and the eel mousse with watercress sauce. Then the pike stuffed with sorrel was disposed of, along with the Bradmenham chicken and truffles baked in a pig's bladder, the Royal Berkshire game pie (with snipe in season) and other serious concerns. Only then did they pause, lean back, and take stock, like travellers leaving a hard road to look at a splendid view. Another bottle was ordered, supplied from a vineyard near Winchester.

'Tomorrow, then,' Mike said.

'I'll drink to that,' said Chris.

Eliot said to Mike, 'You're looking very purposeful.' He turned to Chris. 'Don't you think this man looks full of purpose?'

'Each to his own,' Chris responded, looking cheerful about nothing in particular. 'What are your plans – how is it with you and Aunt Edith?'

'She and I have an appointment for tomorrow, no less.'

'Of course. The holy church of the blessed Saint Alph- Saint Alf- '

'Spot on, mate; Saint Aelfheah. The guy who got biffed to death by Vikings, at a date in the Dark Ages which I shall be at liberty to reveal once I've looked it up again. An excellent chap. By which I mean not only did auntie do a watercolour of his church, but also that 'Plenitude' Figg, blood of my blood – and hers – did a splendid statue of him there. Both works – as you will be free to perceive if you wish – are totally spiffing.'

'A splendid place altogether,' said Mike, as if daring anyone to contradict him. 'And if you don't mind, Monty and I would like to join you there.'

There was a beat's worth of silence. Eliot said, 'Sure. Great idea.'

Mike left shortly afterwards to go to the loo. In his absence the others unthinkingly dropped their voices.

Eliot said, 'You coming too? Tomorrow?'

'If that's okay.'

'He knows where we're going, right?'

'Sure. He said as much, this morning.' Each was mindful of the last time they'd visited St Aelfheah's church, for Mike's wedding to Anna. Chris, bearded and hairy, had been so young, his suit hadn't looked borrowed so much as pilfered.

'Is that why he looks the way he does?' Eliot said.

'Psyching himself up –'

'Like he wants to come top with some holiday task.'

'Would be just like him.'

'I won't say anything if you don't.'

'Yeah, leave it to him, in his own time. If he wants.'

Seeing Mike return, Chris changed the subject. 'And Aunt Edith – ?'

'Yes, indeed,' Eliot responded. 'Aunt Edith. Uh – ?'

'Things are okay between her and you, I take it?'

'Auntie and I are totally cool. Nearly every detail of her life is now present and marshalled. Including the ex-rabble of footnotes. Altogether a splendid woman. Of course it's inconvenient of her to have been dead so long. But scholarly research aside, I dare venture that few women have given any of us such an easy time of it. Even all my exes, to each and every one of whom I drink …I know what you're thinking' – with a pause for another sip of Armanac. 'What you're both thinking of is Marina –'

'No – no –'

'No such woman was in my thoughts –'

'I,' Eliot insisted, 'can think very kindly of Marina –'

'Kindlier than ever – ?' said Chris.

'You may both – either of you – say what you like. But, yes. I can think even kindlier of her now. Because I have decided what to do, when we get to town – to London, which as your cousin Imogen said only the other day, is the place where we go to be grown-ups ... I digress ...'

'Like, not thinking kindly at all,' Mike said, 'of her offspring. Her heir, descendant –'

' – Aftercomer, successor, residuum –'

'Yes – her progeny, issue, scion. Sooner rather than late, I shall see to it that the boy Roland will be enabled. I mean, by being put in a position to utilise resources of his own devising.'

'Empowering him, bigod. No more undermining his self-respect with gifts of money – sorry: with long-term loans.'

'Too right. As for Aunt Edith, I raise my glass to her – and to her worthy forebears and mine –'

'To Augustus 'Plenitude' Figg –'

'And, um, Will, the bargee scribe of Isleworth –'

' – All of whom have been so helpful – and continue to be – as I shin up the north face of the damn thesis. History is – and I defy any man present to contradict me – an ever-changing frame around our own life –'

'No,' said Mike, tipping dangerously back on his chair as he stretched his long legs. 'That's not what it is. History is what you build on. It's an underpinning for what you plan next.'

'History,' Chris put in, sensing a swerve towards Mike's private life, 'is, or should be, a controlled substance.' So soon after the standoff with his aunt, he too couldn't help taking the subject personally. 'Which is why sometimes we should treat it as a joke: precisely because it's not ...'

The bill came, presented as if conferring the freedom of a great city. The total was no more than expected, which is to say massive enough to provoke a general laugh, part nervous, part squiffed. They paid up and walked, more carefully than any man when sober, out of the candlelit restaurant into sudden coolness and country dark.

'Gentlemen,' Chris said, 'the night is ageing and what we have to say will cease to shine. This time, let's not lose the boat.'

XXIII

Far back does she bear us into history, this sweetly sequestered church dedicated to the English martyr St Aelfheah. She was Saxon before she was Norman; and the passing ages have but enhanced her, leaving of themselves more than something made by human hands: a spirit of eternity, no less. He who enters here in search of Art will find marvels indeed, and wondrous it is to see and reflect, in this holy place, upon the melding of the centuries in successive works of piety.

... And where shall we find aught to surpass Augustus 'Plenitude' Figg's statue of St Aelfheah himself at the instant of martyrdom? The saint is garbed here not as his countrymen would have known him in that distant time, but classically robed in the serene splendour of the Augustan Age, as the invading Danes put him to death ...

The King's England: Wessex, Arthur Mee, 1936

They'd expected to sleep well that night, rising relaxed but alert, refreshed, and at ease with themselves and the world. Unluckily they'd moored close to a thicket of willow bushes; so that ruled out a lot of sleep, not to say fellow feeling with the local wildlife. Throughout the hours of darkness the damned nightingales were shouting their heads off right by the boat. Why, thought Eliot, punching his pillow, didn't they stick to their appointed place in the human imagination? Say, two hundred yards off in some beech wood, safely making one's own species ache with thoughts of all-consuming, to-perish-for sex? When the little sods carried on like this, a metre or so distant and higher than your bunk, they just sounded fierce and shrill, with you no more than some species of edible insect.

But the early-summer dawn must have silenced them, since everyone was fathoms deep in sleep when the outside of the hull started resounding, with a dull, repetitive boom. Like most mysteries its explanation proved ordinary: a family of half-grown swans was tearing off fragments of weed from just below the waterline. Around now Chris and Mike decided to give up on sleep, and got dressed; then set about driving the *Speedwell* through the nearest locks before the day's first queue of boats.

Eliot, returning below, was lured back into his bunk, then rendered unconscious, by a passing thought of just-ten-minutes-more. So it was that he, of all people, forgot a foremost example of boating's many Rules Number One: don't go through an emptying lock with the louvres on your window wide open.

A lock chamber with walls in perfect repair would

have been harmless. But this one's masonry was deeply crevassed. As the exit gates swung open, the waters duly surged forward into the river's next reach. They also issued forth from every crack in the sides of the lock: dribbles of a fluid ounce or so from openings no wider than an augur hole, squirtings of a couple of pints from narrow ferny cracks, and, from deep indentations needing serious work, icy jets of a gallon or two. One of these came sluicing through the gaps in a window and soaked Eliot's pillow through to the underside. A fragment of time elapsed, measurable only by internationally funded science, between this incursion and Eliot sitting upright in his bunk with a howl of shock on finding one of his ears filled up with what felt like meltwater.

It was in a convalescent state that the crew breakfasted; and the *Speedwell* puttered rather than powered down to her next mooring. A long shallow valley led from this point on the river, up to a skyline beyond which stood St Aelfheah's.

The church itself promised to be a kind of reliquary, one that held the very soul of composite Englishness, growing and burnished through the centuries. At least, that's what it said in Eliot's copy of Arthur Mee.

'Yes,' said Chris as they eventually arrived, 'but is the history so cool because it's ours, or vice versa?'

Eliot leaned his bike against the churchyard's flinty wall and gave him a glance but said nothing. The eight-mile ride up the valley, with Monty scampering alongside on a lead, had made everyone conscious of his hangover.

St Aelfheah's as a whole may have conjured the essence

of permanence. But its memorials largely described reversals and fresh starts, each in its time a fleeting modern certainty. The list of parish priests celebrated more than one regime change. At the Conquest men with names like Alfwold, Herefrith, and Liafwine had been replaced in an instant with a Norman succession of Hughs, Geoffreys and Rogers; and under the Tudors one incumbent, out of step with the smartly alternating loyalties of his day, had got taken off to Smithfield in 1554 to be ceremonially burned to death. Jacobean Will Fowler the Bargee had described how the church, at a distance from the village it served, had ornamented his noble patron's estate ('Where Art and Nature now as one we see'), like some kind of garden folly. Just over a century later the same baronet's descendant had graciously deployed 'Plenitude' Figg to imply that all of history had been Baroque, in sculpting St Aelfheah's alleged last moments as a luscious up-to-the-minute composition of marble draperies. To signify that he was pelted to death with ox bones, the saint, dignified and prayerful, was shown with an elegantly rendered bovine skull at his feet like an heraldic device. With the railway's arrival in the valley, there came proposals to restore the church 'to a time when all was finest in the medieval mind'. This would have gained it a huge spire and the look of somewhere in a new Victorian suburb; fortunately the money ran out before work could begin.

In her own day Aunt Edith had been too obscure for her *Pastoral Prospect*, featuring the church's exterior, to get a mention from Arthur Mee or any of the other books Eliot had brought along in his pannier bags. Her watercolour made St Aelfheah's look scarcely man made. Rather, it seemed at one with the fields and trees and clouds as just another semi-abstract surface existing, where the artist was concerned, only to reflect light. In modern times some found the resulting work as religious-minded, in its pantheistic way, as any other piece of art to do with this place.

The church's interior certainly didn't lack for solemn monuments, mostly to property and worldly power. Amid so much highly wrought deference it was almost a relief to come across a freak of artistry like the famous effigy to the Countess of Wessex, another patron of the Bargee Poet. In the fashion of the time her ladyship's mortal remains were represented with a frankness that couldn't be surpassed if her bones, emerging putrid through collapsed grave clothes and tattered skin, had been laid out there for real. Some appearances had been kept up; this was a two-decker monument, whose topmost effigy showed the Countess wearing her best in-your-face ruff and farthingale, dignified or what, as if not even dead. Just lying there for show, to demonstrate that she at least was enough of a dude to commission a likeness as frank in the face of death as the ruinous one immediately below.

But if this was supposed to reconcile you to your own mortality, thought Chris, it looked about as helpful as some of the supposed cures for a hangover. His own, this morning, was enough to make thoughts of death neither here nor there. Ignoring the image of the Countess' gristly remains, he put his all into not thinking of raw egg in cayenne pepper; vile enough even without any overlooked fragment of shell. Likewise eggs lightly poached and served in warm hollandaise; a recipe surely designed for ultimate desperation, to help void you once and for all.

Along with his muzzy head and downgraded brain there came thronging memories from their untroubled shared youth, filling the damn place with ghosts. A hundred and twenty such spectres, he calculated, counting the pews, all of which had been full at Mike and Anna's marriage ceremony. Worse, their wedding day had been one of the most cheerful he'd known; not just full of hope for the future but celebrating a courtship that deserved to be crowned with success.

Their combined silence on the subject was growing too loud to be ignored. While both his friends were in earshot, Chris said to Mike, 'This place can't have changed much since we were here last.' Eliot, photographing an inscription on the Countess' tomb, looked up, ready to say something equally anodyne.

'I don't remember much.' If Mike was frowning, it was only from the effort of recall. 'The day went off well enough. But I never noticed that much about the church.' For a man later to distinguish himself in combat, in fact he'd been extraordinarily nervous. On being greeted outside the south door by his brother Alan, the best man, Mike had responded with a confused stare of non-recognition.

'It was the same for me,' Chris put in. 'When getting spliced,'

'Me too,' said Eliot. 'Every time.'

They had the sense to leave it at that, before sounding like ill-assorted guests at a party who knew they wouldn't get on. Mike went off and made a circuit inside the little thick-walled church, with deliberate slowness. He was careful to look at everything, even though a feeling for antique church furnishing was as lacking in him as in one of Thomas Cromwell's commissioners, sent to decapitate every holy image within reach. Afterwards he strolled towards the others, and mentioned Monty's need to be untied and exercised; he'd see them back at the mooring.

All of them knew that once he was gone, his friends would swap a look of relief. He left the bike where it was and untied Monty; then, one striding, the other gleefully lolloping, together they set out up the lane. Mike knew this place hadn't left him untouched; only a fool would pretend that what happened here, a generation ago, hadn't really taken place. But why else had he'd volunteered to come along, if not to tidy such memories into their place? Presumably the exercise had been a success, since now, his gesture made, all he felt was a spreading numbness. Meanwhile the prompt efficiency central to his nature reasserted itself. Never mind what he was expected to feel on revisiting this scene from another life; such expectations had nothing to do with his personal truth to self. If the world thought that he – *he* – could be unsettled by its own weight of ignorance and preconception, then it was wrong.

XXIV

Say, shall we...ascend,
While radiant Summer opens all its pride,
Thy hill, delightful Shene? Here let us sweep
The boundless landscape; now the raptured eye,
Exulting, swift to huge Augusta send...
To lofty Harrow now, and now to where
Majestic Windsor lifts his princely brow
In lovely contrast to this glorious view,
Calmly magnificent, then will we turn
To where the silver Thames first rural grows?

The Seasons: Summer, James Thomson (1700-1748)

There are many ways of knowing that a great city lies over the horizon. It depends what route you take. A rolling landscape of farms and fields may find itself bestrode by converging lines of pylons. Or the first large golf course hints that several million people live just out of sight. From the outermost suburbs uneven concentric rings lie around London: at twenty miles, the encircling M25; at fifteen or so, near the first shaded suburban streets, riding schools multiply. Cemeteries and giant malls spread themselves about eight miles out; and towards the edge of the congestion-charge zone the largest features include marshalling yards, cold-storage depots, throughway interchanges, and one or two world-famous teaching hospitals, each a city in its own right.

Entering London down the river is not like that. Even here the world goes on standing back from the Thames. Of course there are changes. Water meadows are replaced by sports fields, or by the suburban park around a great house once twenty river miles out of town in deep Middlesex countryside. The towpath is still overhung with trees, but now becomes thick with dog-walkers and enough bicycles for any street in Amsterdam or Leyden. Where flooding can threaten only the bottom quarter acre of lawn, villas from the lost era of steam-launches and day trippers can be glimpsed, often with a matching Edwardian boathouse.

Unseen beneath the waters thrashed by passing craft, all kinds of archaeology lie undiscovered, as in a winding two-hundred-mile burial site. From Gloucestershire, through a green landscape too low-lying for villages or country lanes, all the way down to London and the sea, the river goes on yielding fragments by the thousand from sites of pagan sacrifice: flint axes, Bronze age swords. Nearer the metropolis the city is perceived as a rumour of itself – say, as a distant alteration in the sky where the clouds above it have thickened – and here too the debris changes on the river bed. As elsewhere much survives – ceremonial sickles, palstaves, ornamental harness – that was cast into the water as an offering to river deities or gods of battle. But even more comes from recent centuries, fallen there by accident in the course of ordinary life.

With a day to go before they planned to pass Tower Bridge and disembark at St Catherine's Dock, the *Speedwell* sailed past Sunbury and the house where Mike had lived before. Before, that is, yielding to his destiny and moving to the houseboat with Bianca and the twins. Even here in this bland suburban riverscape of mown lawns and flowering ornamental trees, out beyond their former garden's wobbly little landing stage there lay undiscovered beneath the passing tourist boats a nineteenth-century clay pipe, a broken souvenir mug from the coronation of Edward VII, an eighty-year-old pushchair and a silver fish-knife, together with a toy vacuum flask lost by young Sam while playing at explorers in the family's dinghy.

Mike was at the wheel as they went past. Instinctively he kept his eyes on the river traffic ahead; it had taken some days to get used to the fact that a boat had no brakes. A mile further on he and some troublesome other self started debating. Why, it demanded, should he have avoided a sideways look at his no-longer home? Well, why not, demanded his 'real' self. The only way to resolve this, after they'd moored for the night near Hampton Wick, was to get into the dinghy and row back upriver to see how he really felt. It would be an excellent way to stiffen his resolution of several days back, and ensure that nothing stood between him and being a good husband to the wife that he, an upright man of independent views, had chosen of his own accord.

It was in this frame of mind that he set himself to phone Lisbon before he got into the dinghy. It was earlier than usual – from a thousand miles away he'd grown used to calling at times that fitted around the twins' pattern of feeding and sleep, after one or two conversations with Bianca had been terminally disrupted by infantine shrieks for attention. Better to be early, though, than taking an incoming call in the dinghy, maybe losing an oar while he fumbled for the phone. Or while drifting in front of some overbearing cabin cruiser like an ugly mansion built of Tupperware. Or just dropping the phone into a puddle at the bottom of the boat.

For privacy's sake he left the *Speedwell* and got out onto the towpath. Most calls were easier when walking up and down; and no one out of earshot could guess what was being said so long as you remembered to stick your other hand in a pocket and not gesticulate.

The phone was answered by an unknown female voice: elderly, non-English-speaking; maybe some dependant cousin or family servant. After a brief wait he was passed on to Bianca's mother, as the household's presiding force.

His mother-in-law had recently ceased to speak to him in anything but Portuguese. Bianca claimed that this must be an expression of respect for his improved mastery of the language. Either that, he thought with a momentary flicker of disloyalty, or it was felt he should be made to practise more.

In English for once however, Mrs Pereira said, 'Oh, it's you.'

He assumed that in Portuguese her meaning must surely sound more hospitable.

She added, 'Here is my daughter, who I know will have important things to say to you.'

'Hello, Michael,' Bianca said. 'How are you?' Without waiting for an answer she asked, 'And how is the big boat of your friend progressing?'

'It progresses well, thank you. As do I.'

'Are you near London yet?' There was a small pause, as if someone had signalled at her; then she continued, 'My family and friends are all very interested to hear of your boat's journey.'

'Yes, we've already reached the beginnings of London. This evening finds us near Hampton Court Palace, and tomorrow afternoon we hope to finish our journey by the Tower of London.'

The worst of it was, he could hear himself speaking like a poorly programmed robot. The sooner they were together, independent of the damn phone, the sooner everything would be fine. He willed it so; for God's sake, wasn't that enough?

'And, Michael, do please tell me: where exactly are you? Because when I asked you yesterday you said you and your friends would be driving Eliot's boat past the town called Sunbury. At least, that's where the map said you would go. And I think we can all see your journey too on Google Earth. Have you been to that town yet?'

Until their last conversation Mike had forgotten much of their shared confidences in the first days and nights of knowing each other. Lured on by the rightness of sharing every personal detail, and encouraged by her rapt attention, he'd obeyed the impulse to describe every aspect of his home.

'Well, yes –'

'And so did you see the house? We know you would have passed next to it, in your friend's boat.'

'Yes, but –'

'So what did it look like? Has your – Have there been any changes?'

'We were driving the boat straight past; it was hard to see anything much.'

There was more silence at the other end, interspersed with whispering.

'But there would have been a for sale sign. Surely there must have been one of those.'

'Anna sold the house very quickly. There'll be someone else living there now.'

'I have difficulty in believing that it could have been sold so quickly. If there is no for sale sign, could that mean it has not yet been put onto the market?'

'Believe me, it was sold the first week it was advertised.'

'But did you not pay for the house yourself? Entirely with money of your own?'

'Yes. But there were reasons for that.'

'They cannot have been very great ones. What kind of reasons? Did the person who you were married to, back then – did she not help you expedite these important things, like buying that house?'

'Bianca, what are you trying to say?' Mike was genuinely confused.

'Because if you paid for the house in the beginning, surely it has always been yours alone. So if it has been sold, there would have been more money.'

For a moment he really had no idea what to say. He'd told her everything about his finances; without sharing every detail, it wouldn't be a marriage. And now something else besides confusion was inhibiting him. For the first time, he found there was much of his earlier life that he didn't want to share. Correction, whispered some innermost angel or demon; you don't want to share it with her. You don't want her anywhere near those times.

In a low, inflexible voice he said, 'I know I told you that we split everything by shared agreement: fifty-fifty. If we'd gone through the courts there would have been almost no money at all. I told you that. I remember you said that you understood.'

From back on deck, Monty lifted first his ears, then his head from where it rested on his forepaws. Not having heard Mike sound like this before, he looked on warily.

One of the things Mike had told Bianca he most valued in her was that she knew her own mind. In the early weeks her admiration for him – 'my marvellous brave soldier' – had appeared so heartfelt, he hadn't stopped to think how it would feel to oppose her in any way…

She said, 'I do not think her lawyers can have been honest with you. A house like that is a more valuable thing than you understand, Michael. Otherwise half of everything would come to much more than you now tell me you have.'

Carefully, as if trying against great odds not to drop

and break something fragile, he said, still in the same pent-up voice, 'I wish we'd had this exchange of views before, since it will be – it is – absolutely necessary for you to understand what I've just said.'

His words might have perished and evaporated in mid-air. She replied, 'My mother says that my cousin, who is an attorney, says you should appeal, if the money is unsatisfactory. My family are all agreed with him: it is what you should do, to assert yourself against people who have no claim.'

Lost for words? Him? He wasn't just speechless: he didn't know himself. With the phone still pointlessly held to his ear, Mike twisted several times where he stood, hither and thither. He glimpsed Eliot on deck taking an enquiring look and struggled to collect himself.

'Bianca.' He didn't usually call her by name; they'd mostly used whimsically coded endearments. 'Neither of us – not me, not you – should argue by phone. I can't tell you' – he was breathing deeply like a half-drowned swimmer coming up for air – 'I can't – I cannot – tell you, but you must understand, how important this is. It's something that should only ever be done face to face. Please tell me you understand that.'

'I understand that, Michael; of course I do. But I still know what I know. We must speak properly of such things when we meet again next month.'

'Next month – ?' He was too dismayed to recall if this, whatever date she'd originally meant, was when Bianca had said she'd return. Nor had he the heart just then to ask. Their call ended soon after, rather politely.

*

Half an hour later Mike shipped the oars and tied up the dinghy to a ring on the so familiar landing stage. He hadn't been fit to see or speak to his friends. In fact his call to Bianca had left him so angry he could scarcely have been content to face down an enemy. His prized power of reasoning, so called, was nowhere; without a thought he'd got into the boat and rowed back up the river to his former home.

No way was he fit to reason why he'd come here. An honest self-appraisal might have shown that all he wanted was to be somewhere unconnected with his present life. From the waterline next to the jetty, he could see all the way up the garden. The house, banal and comfortable, had been built a hundred years ago, with gables and dorky half-timbering, and white-painted French windows giving onto a broad patio.

He found himself scrutinizing every detail, willing everything to be unchanged. The tree house he'd built for his children was intact, though the ladder was missing a rung. Also someone had overdone it when cutting back the big ceananthus by the path round to the front; in full bloom, Sam once said, it was so blue, it was like a patch of alternative reality burning through. There were still toys on the patio: a red and yellow plastic tricycle, and a child's first real bike, lying on its side. If it was time travel he sought, there should also be music practice audible from beyond an open window. First stages of learning the violin, perhaps, or infantine tootling on a recorder.

Mike sat hunched in the boat with no purpose he knew of, hands clasped, forearms resting across his knees, looking down at nothing. If he listened hard, it was just possible to hear someone playing a piano. Just right, too. Which was to say, with no more nor less ability than his children had shown. From the stops and starts it could be Jessie herself, sitting up very straight and, at twelve years old, improbably serious about everything.

But the tune was wrong. He recognized it, but not as anything his own children had been set to play. Its unfamiliarity, in this context, spoiled everything. What the hell was he doing here, anyway?

Up at the house, a dog had just been let out into the garden. An Old English sheepdog, larger than Monty and far less disciplined. It bounded towards him; reaching the bank it bounced from side in frustration, half inclined to wag its tail, but barking loudly nonetheless. From outside the house a man shouted at the dog, and hurried across the lawn to silence it.

'Excuse me,' he said to Mike, 'but are you lost?'

Mike indicated something amounting to no. It occurred to him that he, on this very spot, had had several encounters with people who, like him now, at first sight might have been trespassers.

'I know sometimes this has been mistaken for a pub garden.' The man indicated a so-familiar three-seater wooden bench and a marble-topped table with matching Victorian-style garden chairs. They stood on an area of York stone paving that Anna had commissioned so that in warm weather they could sup at the water's edge. It gave Mike a moment's surprise that he could recall buying them.

'Yes,' he said, 'I expect it has. More often than you'd think.' Only now did he remember how he must look, with his half-grown beard and general end-of-holiday slovenliness.

The man made no reply. Householder and guard dog stood above him, waiting.

'I'm sorry,' he lied, looking up at them. 'I just had to, uh, pull over to take a call.'

'That's fine.'

'You're very kind ...' So saying, he untied the boat and rowed slowly away, into the silver waters and pale rose sky of a perfectly splendid midsummer sunset.

X X V

London, thou art the flower of cities all!
Gemme of all joy, jasper of jocunditie…

William Dunbar (1465?-1530?)

But why this bit of verse? Chris wondered. With all the other stuff to quote from; say, Wordsworth, clichéd or not, what had made him think of these lines? I mean, jasper me no jocundities; seriously, Will. Not in a time and place that look like this.

The *Speedwell* was passing under Westminster Bridge and it was raining. Last night, hot and damp as unrisen bread, everyone had slept face up and starfish shaped, arms and legs out wide in an instinctive quest for coolness. All around them, from the western suburbs on in, eight or nine million other people had maybe lain spread-eagled in the selfsame pose. Today's change in the weather had been sudden enough to see the *Speedwell*'s crew piling on sweaters over sunburned gooseflesh as one man.

Now, in the last two miles before St Catherine's Dock, it was time to take their voyage seriously, with only Eliot possessing the confidence and practical knowledge to take the wheel. However metropolitan the river had become, from here it was also an arm of the sea. The currents were stronger, the tides higher and deeper; and the shores were just beginning their retreat from each other. The tide was in, with the Houses of Parliament rising like a mighty vessel at anchor, a fantastical ship of state in a never-was style of Gothic. But London in general didn't look like anywhere celebrated in verse. In fact it didn't much resemble any version of itself, being almost blanked out by the weather. After weeks of drought the rain was in earnest: not the violent sousing you'd expect from a thunderstorm or a carwash, nor the deceptively fine, all-penetrating drizzle of a Scotch mist. This was proper, steady rain that seeped into your eyes and ran, freezing cold, inside your collar; rain falling as though no other kind of weather existed.

Of course visibility wasn't as bad as in a London particular, the pea-souper fog of old newsreels. But the cloud was low, so that in the City a convocation of new Brutalist towers looked even taller for being topless, each summit obscured. Only the Shard, ghosting into view, was diminished, taking the form of a flat-topped pyramid scarcely three hundred feet high. The all-enveloping greyness rendered most shapes vague; whenever another vessel approached, a river bus or freighted barge, it was the only moving thing in sight. The curtain of rain was a vast screen, onto which the imagination could project any city it liked: Whistler's mysterious Victorian Thames by night, in mood-infused strokes of silver and purplish-black; or the crowded river of Canaletto's London, all space and light and elegance beneath a Venetian sky of cerulean blue as if viewing the city's glittering vista through the eye of a benign divinity.

At Tower Bridge the roadway was raised and parted: two thin semaphoring arms. Pass, they said, mainly to an ocean-going yacht registered in Dubai and twice the size of any wooden man o' war, being crewed up the river to a berth in Chelsea. After the bridge's fanciful great turrets and the glimpse of widening river beyond, the lock chamber into St Catherine's Dock felt as confining as a burrow. The *Speedwell* edged into her mooring, in a deserted townscape of restored brick warehouses, shops, restaurants, a new hotel building, and cafes with their pavement life rained off. On fine days this place resembled a stage set thronged with chorus members; after time spent idling beneath an open sky it was strange in any weather to be surrounded by a close horizon made of roofs.

As always after a day on the river, when the engine had been cut, the silence that followed was loud enough to suggest its own echo. In the galley, beneath the drumming of rain, they looked at each other, sighed aloud, felt sad and pleased. Was this a moment when someone should say something? A memorable one-liner, perhaps. Or even a speech of thanks to Eliot, as their captain. Later, maybe.

Now that they were back in the world, they supposed they'd all have to get on with life's unfinished business. Starting, for Chris, not many hours hence at St Martin's in the Fields. It was strange to think that next time they met, each of them would be wearing a suit.

XXVI

Step One: Enhancing Your Essence

... Say you've just come back from holiday. Maybe this has been a precious time, leading you into the right space, an interlude of gracefulness empowering you to live as you deserve. The door has opened for you, into an authentic life, one that is congruent with your need for self-actualization.

And now you're back home. You know what you have to do, right? Because this is not a return to the life of spiritual drudgery and dull-eyed self-sabotage. Now you know to approach each moment with trust, confident that your existence need no longer be shaped by external forces. Moreover, those around you will be moved to follow, ready like you to honour the synchronicities in life.

Here's the first step you can take to defend your priceless core of peacefulness.

Close the door on the outside world, kick off your shoes, and put your wristwatch where you can't see *it. Now, take out the collection you have made of souvenirs for private quiet times: a gull's feather perhaps, or a ticket to a movie you enjoyed, or a verse of poetry written by you for your eyes alone ... All these will help you to a new respect for the existential purity of solitude...*

'How to Be Truly Great: Revealing the True You',
Dr F. Lucette Bamburger, Dip. Phil., Dip. CS, TSD

Next to a copy of Dr Bamburger's latest on self-help, in Marina's sitting room the phone rang. It was a retro device in the style of seventy years ago, the receiver placed crosswise above a dial. Unfortunately it weighed less than any original and shifted all over the place if you tried to get a number using one hand. Its ornamentation was gilt, aimed at Rococo pastiche.

'Roly! Darling, how are you! What's your news? Are you alright ...?'

'Yes Ma. Of course I am.'

'Well, that's wonderful, darling, so ...? You did get the money all right?'

'Yes, thanks –'

'Oh, I'm so glad!'

'In fact it's about that –'

'Why? Is there some problem?'

'No, Ma. I just said everything's okay.'

'I'm sorry, darling. What were you going to tell me?'

'I was going to say, I think I can come to the church after all.'

'Oh, but that's wonderful! I know no one will mind. I mean, a memorial service isn't like a wedding, is it? And I'm sure you'll be glad you came. An occasion like this – well, one could meet all sorts of people.'

'You did tell me Eliot would be there. And I'd rather say the needful face to face.'

'You mean, to thank him?'

'Well, yes, Ma. What did you think I meant?'

'Oh Roly! That's so sweet of you. But – darling, I hope you don't mind me saying this – I know he'll be so pleased that you're grateful towards him. Only, I don't think he'd like you to mention it directly.'

'So how would he like me to mention it?'

'Oh, I know you'll think of some way to show him how you feel. I mean, without being too, what shall I say, forthright? After all, he never came straight out and said it was for you. It's our little secret, you see – his and mine. What happened, the last time I spoke to him, was that he asked how much you needed, you know, for …'

'Yes Ma. We know why I needed it.'

'Yes – sorry, darling. Anyway, the subject changed, I forget to what, and then, right at the end, he said he'd send the money – I mean, the amount we'd just been talking about – but that it was a birthday present for myself. Or, he said, maybe it would help me get the roof fixed. And I was just about to say, But I don't have responsibility for the roof, when – well, it dawned on me what he'd really meant.'

'So he doesn't want me to mention it at all?'

'Not in so many words, I think.'

'You mean, in case he doesn't feel like following up with anything more? Any time later?'

'Actually he did mention that.'

'He did? Really?'

'No – no – not like that. Roly, darling, you don't know him the way I do –'

'Ma, what are you talking about?'

'I'm sorry – what I mean is that Eliot can be very… well, not ruthless – that's not what I mean – but – oh, not implacable, exactly – perhaps adamant is the word I want. Absolutist, maybe. You'd understand too, if you'd ever overheard him conducting business.' Marina knew well enough that Eliot's soft heart could co-exist with any degree of hard-headedness.

'Right … Adamant about what?'

'Oh, about ever expecting anything more. And when he says something like that – I'm sorry to have say this – but I know he does mean it. Oh – and Roly – I'm so sorry about the job. Eliot was quite definite about that too – says he's decided on an internal promotion, I'm afraid. I know what a disappointment that must be for you. I really do, darling.'

'Never mind that. There's really no need to talk about it.'

'Why? Has something else come up? How wonderful that would be – do tell!'

He ignored her. Sounding as nearly earnest as he ever did, he said, 'Look, there's something I want to hand over to you.'

'Oh, darling, you shouldn't!' Like him, she hadn't forgotten that her birthday fell later that week. 'But if you want to give it to me personally, why don't I save you any trouble and come round to your apartment?' She dared not add, *so I can actually see this mysterious place, to be sure you're looking after yourself properly.*

'No need for that. I'll come to your place.'

'Oh, but really – you'll have to go out of your way …'

'No I won't. Besides, I've lent the flat to some friends. Just for a few days.'

'That's very generous of you. Anybody – no; I mean, sorry – sorry, darling. Of course they won't be anyone I know …But – can't you just give it to me at the church?'

'No. That won't do.' Roland was thinking that if Eliot was serious about withholding any future finances, turning up at the church to see what more might be done with him would be a waste of time. He said, 'There is one thing. After I've given it to you, promise you won't sneak a look inside.'

She laughed delightedly. 'Oh, why?'

'That would seriously – I mean, seriously – spoil everything. I want to be there when it's opened. I'm sure you can promise me that.'

'Darling, of course I do. You know you can always count on me.'

*

Martha's phone rang. She was with her sister and brother-in-law, finishing a pot of coffee in the conservatory of their house in Barnes. Seeing it was Chris, she took the call in the garden.

'Hi. I'm back.'

'I think I know what you mean. You haven't all just moored at the end of the road, have you?'

'Of course not. I wasn't going to let the chaps make their entry into town without me. For what it was worth...'

'How are you?'/'All well?' he and Martha asked at once. Chris added, 'Is Imogen with you?'

'She was, earlier.'

'She's not staying with her mother? I thought she said she'd rather die.'

'No, that's not what I meant. She's just gone out. With Tom, to see a movie.'

'Nothing too taxing?'

'A romcom. She said she'd take him along; her treat. I think he's a bit overawed. He's never seen her in nearly-grown-up mode.'

There was a pause, like the turning of a page in a ceremonial book. He said, 'Did you always know something I didn't? About my cousin?'

'Certainly not.' Sometimes no one could match Martha's snap of finality. But then no part of her nature was gracefully retiring. Let alone given to avoiding awkwardnesses, for everyone's sake.

She added, 'How could I have? In that sort of case. Even as a professional.'

'Don't expect me to forgive myself.' Said fiercely, as in contradiction.

'None of that.' Likewise inflexible.

Another pause. Then Martha said, 'You had no business being anything but innocent.' See it this way, she thought. I even love you for your errors – well, some of the less idiotic ones. You had to believe in the people who fostered you – how else was a lost boy to thrive, growing up in a dark place?

Maybe one day she'd feel free to say it out loud.

Chris said nothing. He wanted to tell her – not now; later, to her face – that he'd not have been so lucky in marriage, if he'd been a different man. Another great escape.

Hearing him lost for words, Martha turned the conversation. '…Oh, and Leonora's been on at me –'

'About my eulogy? What did you say?'

'I said, I'm convinced there'll be nothing in it to upset your cousin.'

'I made sure there wouldn't be – I called Imogen, yesterday.'

'And …?'

'She said, "If there's no fucking in it, poor Mummy will be so pleased."'

*

Mike could hear the phone ringing and ringing, in Lisbon. That particular ring tone, neutral in itself, had become freighted with associations he'd rather not name.

A female voice. But no – not her. His mother-in-law.

He identified himself, answering in English. The tone of his last conversation with Bianca, and the hours that had passed meanwhile, now left him unequal to using a second language.

Without preliminaries he demanded, 'Is Bianca there?' Pleasantries too, had deserted him.

'I see for you,' Mrs Pereira said, also in English though without indicating that she recognized him. A near-silence followed. He strained to hear if there were voices in the background. A small child was somewhere at hand, talking infantine scribble as if trying out syllables before graduating to words. Almost certainly Portuguese-only scribble by now, he thought.

'She is not free – she is not here to speak to you.'

'Will you please find out from my wife when she will be in a position to speak to me?'

'Yes.'

'What?'

'I will find out. When she is here to speak.'

'I need to know when she's coming back – coming home. I need her to tell me that.'

'I said. I find out.'

The line went dead.

He'd have been even angrier, if there hadn't been other recent calls like this.

XXVII

A Service of Thanksgiving for the Life and
Achievements of

HUGH DENHOLM LOVELL, OBE, MSc, PhD,
FRCP, FRCPsych, Emeritus Professor of
Psychological Medicine

Sure enough they hardly knew each other. Haircuts had
been had and Mike's incipient beard was shaved off. Eliot
in particular found his waistband tightened. Before they
were due at St Martin's there were drinks and canapes in a
suite at the Savoy for a select three dozen mourners, most
of them contacts and friends of Leonora. She was damned
if she'd fumble this chance to round up all that was most
impressive in her address files, just because some people
were so important and terribly busy that they couldn't
make it to the church.

The gathering was in a space that demanded to be
called a venue rather than just part of a suite. It wasn't

extraordinarily spacious, but it seemed unbounded. Not only did its huge window overlook the Thames, but every wall was floor-to-ceiling mirrored. The effect dazzled. Now that a shower had cleared and the sun shone, a torrent of light appeared to flow all around the room. One almost expected the floor to pitch gently as if riding at anchor.

Leonora's starriest guests were mostly though not all identifiable as famous faces. Family members were also present, as were certain friends of family who could be counted on to fill the corners of the room in a seemly fashion and talk among themselves. Champagne was served by stonkingly pretty waitresses, every one of whom Chris suspected of being overqualified.

'At bashes like this I half expect to be served by one of my PhD graduates.'

'It's what happens in a recession. Bar staff and people get literate, and they get better looking.' Mike spoke in the flat tones of someone absent when present. His current look of dourness was unlike anything his friends thought of as his true self. Near the door Monty lay like a downbeat doggy avatar, head resting on his front paws, eyes roaming the room; the best-behaved guest of them all. Even if the houseboat in Twickenham hadn't started feeling derelict, Mike wouldn't have had the heart to leave him tied up there all day.

Imogen was the brightest person in the room, at least sartorially. The dress code for the church service had been described as celebratory. She'd responded by turning up in another garment Chris and Martha hadn't seen before, a designer piece in poppy-red silk, with a slender waist and full skirt.

'Did your mother help choose that beautiful frock?' asked one guest, whose husband was the publisher of Leonora's latest book on childcare. She was a literary agent, well respected for her negotiating skills. But like everyone else she felt insecure at not knowing what Imogen's mental state might be. Frankly it was impossible to know what one should say to the poor girl.

'God, no,' replied Imogen. 'Mummy and I couldn't bear to go shopping together. Besides, she doesn't have the time.'

The woman retreated in confusion behind a polite smile. Out of courtesy to Leonora, her husband also felt a duty to speak to Imogen.

'I was so sorry to hear about your father's death,' he ventured. There seemed safety in saying the obvious.

'I wasn't.' Imogen's response was brisk but neutral, as if answering to her name.

'What my daughter means,' put in Leonora, overhearing, 'is that her relationship with Hugh was complex and many-sided –'

'Mummy's got it absolutely right. That's exactly what I was about to say. After all, who can try to understand their relationship with anyone close and not be puzzled? Can they, Mummy?'

Leonora smiled on, while the features of her inner self roiled in confusion and social dread. 'Darling,' she said, as if making a public announcement, 'it makes me very happy to see the person you've become – so confident in your opinions.'

'Oh, bollocks to that, Mumsie. I know it's good of you to say so; I'm not stupid. But once I'm over my last meds, I'm going to practise saying as little as possible. Everyone knows that's how to make people think you're interesting and clever.'

Concerned for the goodwill of Leonora as a celebrity author, her publisher's wife felt obliged to murmur, 'I hope your mother doesn't mind you talking to her like that. She's been through a very difficult time too, you know.' She glanced concernedly at Leonora.

'Of course she has. If there's one thing you can say about our family, we have found ways of being unusually close. Haven't we, Mummy?' Imogen seemed cheerful but calm as she said this. The onset of sanity suits her, thought Martha, looking on.

Not so Leonora. Head lowered in the direction of her ever-disappointing daughter, she darkened, as if about to commit some form of cocktail-party suicide.

'This may not be the moment,' Chris said, stepping between them. 'But Leonora, I do need a private word. About my speech ...' If he'd been the blushing type, the crudeness of his intervention would have turned him a shade of hot pink right down to the gaps between his toes.

Even Chris looking significant was easier for Leonora to bear than her unpredictable daughter. Readily she retreated with him to a corner.

In a confidential voice he said, 'Perhaps you can advise me – I know this is short notice – but I think we need a microphone at the foot of the steps to the pulpit...'

She contrived the inquiring look of someone who

knew it wasn't really her place to speak, all the while eyeing Imogen with the wariness owed to a weapons-grade custard pie.

'…The thing is, I still haven't decided whether to solicit impromptu reminiscences from other members of the congregation. So that everyone can feel they have a part to play…'

Marina entered the party. Head high, eyes uncertain.

At any other time Leonora would have seen off Chris's suggestion, with a few words that united tact with absolute refusal. She'd laboured too hard to choreograph the unrepeatable opportunity of today's ceremony. As it was, in a voice close to meekness she said, 'I know I can trust you, Crispin, to do whatever is best.'

Restored to seeming dignity, she moved away to join her other guests.

'Eliot, darling!'

Like a man suffering an undignified domestic accident, Eliot turned and saw Marina. She wore a too-bright look of sociability. He cursed himself for having mentioned this gathering, as an excuse not to meet her and the boy Roland. 'So that we can all touch base together,' she'd said, 'maybe somewhere nice.'

'I know it's awfully naughty of me to be here; but you will protect me, won't you? It's just that I wanted to apologize to you, for Roly not turning up after all – I've just had a call from him –'

'There's no need to apologise for that.' Now that it was too late to deflect Marina he wasn't surprised to see her here. As her fortunes had shrunk, she'd acquired serious form as a gatecrasher. Give that woman marks for doggedness and pluck, he'd thought.

Though not today. He couldn't resist saying, 'The church service is also invitation only, you know.'

'Oh, surely not. It's just like a funeral, isn't it? I know you don't need an invitation for one of those – I looked it up.' And having secured squatter's rights as she perceived them, in the form of a glass of champagne from a passing waitress, Marina resolutely looked around her, ready to start working the room.

As a stranger to almost everyone, she herself went unnoticed – except by Leonora. Marina, seeing this elegant and distinguished woman looking at her – and, yes, a TV celebrity – she went up and introduced herself.

'I'm with Eliot – I believe he's someone who's known you for years.'

Leonora figured this intruder with a look as brief as the click of a shutter. Used clothing. The accessories too. Several well-dressed men present were wearing a suit once owned by their father. But Marina's contribution to recycling was nowadays more charity shop. Anyone to whom such things mattered, like Leonora, should have been impressed as all hell by how heroically well the woman dressed, on how little. The fact remained that Marina's handbag for example, though genuine crocodile, was not a minor heirloom but in a boxy style that hadn't returned in nearly a lifetime.

Marina held out her hand. 'I've heard so much about you –'

'That's good.' Leonora responded to Marina's proffered

paw with the handshake of social rejection, limp as a piece of fishmonger's defrosted dab. 'And now that you're here among us, let me introduce you to my daughter.'

It didn't happen. Moments after Marina's arrival, there was one individual to whom she became the most interesting person in the room.

Monty rose to his feet and scurried to sit down next to her, plus Roland's package, to be opened only in his presence. His claws clicked on the parquet. Otherwise he seemed not to notice Marina. Instead he aimed an exultant cacophony of barks straight at Mike.

Who said, 'Oh ...shit!'

So Monty's training did extend to illicit pharmaceuticals. What else could he possibly be on about?

'Oh, bugger!' said Eliot. The cause of Monty's ecstatic sounding-off grew in his mind too from a possibility to a likelihood.

Curious and a little annoyed, Marina showed no more response than most people there. Eliot delivered himself of an almighty sigh. Compromised again by this luckless woman's vulnerability. With a look of kindness he took her by the arm.

'Dear Marina ...'

She met his eyes with uncomprehending tenderness. He hadn't spoken to her like that since they were both twenty-four...

'I need,' he said, urgent and intimate, 'to see you outside.'

*

Leonora let herself be soothed by the music. The church's great organ gave forth the sounds of a piece by Handel, in tones resonant enough for stateliness, yet not so loud that anyone's liver or pancreas actually got to vibrate. So far everything had gone to plan. At the drinks party no one seemed to have noticed whatever was going on with the dog, or with that woman. And now, true to herself, her gift for names and faces, and her position as Hugh's widow, she had looked as calm and queenly as one could wish, greeting each mourner as they entered the church.

One rogue thought did flicker into being. What if Imogen had elected to stand there beside her at the west door, free-spoken as a three-year-old parroting its elders? Be grateful for things as they are, she thought while the service progressed. And if there is any hitch today, brace up and remember that none of it will be your fault.

The time came for Chris to ascend the pulpit and speak.

No one, afterwards, made much comment either way. Even Martha was uncertain of what Chris planned to say, though as his speech progressed she was one of very few who knew enough to be astonished. After the first few minutes it was costing her, as she laboured to fake a look of polite not-boredom.

'Many of you here today might have spoken of my uncle more fittingly than I...' As he began his address to the congregation's upturned faces, all the scene lacked was a celestial spotlight via one of the tall windows, a dust-speckled sunbeam directed onto Leonora. It was the least she deserved. As she listened with calm attentiveness to

Chris's every word and intonation, it was as if she couldn't get enough of what he had to say. No one could have held herself with greater dignity: Walter Mitty, smiling as he looked a firing squad in the eye, had nothing on Leonora.

Later, people told each other they'd known that was how she'd look, up there at the front of the nave, her family gathered around her, and she never so strong as now. Leonora had been unsure whether Imogen would agree to sit beside her, along with Martha and Tom. 'You need only join us in front if you want to, darling,' she'd said. 'But some people might be ungenerous if they see we're not all sitting together.'

'Mummy, you know that's crap. No one remembers what I look like, I've been banged up so long.' But she went along with her mother; and even paid close attention to what Chris was saying, leaning forward throughout and not once taking her eyes off his face. By contrast with her mother's massive stoicism, for some reason Imogen looked almost cheerful. As if nothing he said could surprise her.

There did come a point when Leonora could only look straight ahead. By degrees her face had become ashen as she waited in anguished uncertainty to hear what Chris might really have to say.

'It is my duty, however, as one of those who knew him best – who understood him as he really was – to hold up before you the life, in its every extraordinary aspect, of a man perceived as a legend within the field of psychiatric scholarship and practice that he so memorably bestrode...'

It would be too flattering to say that Chris's speech was a model of good judgement, delivered with restraint. Now he was here, he found himself angered on his own account as well as for anyone else whose trust his uncle had betrayed. There were two things on which he was resolved. One: stay believable, by seeming to speak not a word of sarcasm, or even righteous rage. Two, do dishonour to a rogue.

'...It could be said that he was one of the foremost figures of his time – a colossus, indeed – within the profession to which he gave so much. And yet, for all the plaudits received by this remarkable man, who was surely admired by everyone with whom he came into contact, and for all the honours heaped on him in his glittering career, there was yet one thing that meant more to him.' (Significant pause; solemn gaze for all to see, turned upon Leonora.) 'His family, ladies and gentlemen ...Though he would treat every patient as carefully as if they were his own child, it was this that stood at the core of this towering personality ...'

As a man of truth, Chris had never guessed how easy lying could be, when the well-springs of contempt ran quite so deep and full. He even got in a description of Hugh, 'within the field of mental healing where he so famously excelled', as 'a larger-than-life figure'. (Serve the old bastard right – his uncle loathed clichés. Probably his one lonesome little virtue.)

In the end he gave it to them for over half an hour, revelling in the relief of his own cynicism. Eliot, who'd heard him speak in public before, looked on disbelieving at Chris's breach of his usual rules: keep it short and leave them laughing. And so far eleven uses of 'iconic'? Who was this guy in the pulpit, and what had he done with their old friend?

Chris didn't know himself either. Nor did he find he gave a bugger. If everyone here thought his uncle was so great, it served them right, having to sit still for this platitudinous dreckfest. When he actually finished, the congregation surprised him with a round of applause. Maybe they were just relieved to hear him stop.

Leonora was relieved too. As the congregation applauded, she yielded to a cloudburst of sobs. She was helped to the privacy of the vestry by Janet, herself dressed as if for this moment: an attendant character, maybe the confidante in a classical tragedy, correct in black. Everyone sympathized; after so much valorous self-control, how could poor Leonora not collapse at the last, especially after having heard her wonderful husband so respectfully described, and in such detail?

There was one bad moment, as Chris descended from the pulpit. Imogen had hidden her face on Martha's shoulder and was shaking violently. Only after he'd hastened up to them and thrown an urgent look at Martha did he understand.

A helpless fit of the giggles. For the second time since he'd known her as an adult, Imogen was laughing.

XXVIII

Dunkerque May – June 1940

Commemorative plaque, College of Heralds. Issued to
vessels including the *Speedwell*, cabin cruiser

From behind the great glassy face of the hotel above St
Catherine's Dock, one or two onlookers glanced down at
what was happening on board the *Speedwell*. People were
entitled to be mildly curious. A middle-aged man in an
expensive suit and silk tie, surely the boat's owner, was
stooping to polish a piece of brasswork. He wielded a can
of cleaning fluid and a rag as if he didn't even know he
was dressed for a formal occasion: a wedding maybe, or a
public inquiry. But if Eliot had noticed an audience, he still
wouldn't care what they thought. Even his friends didn't
tease him whenever he went out of his way to polish up
the boat's memorial plaque, with its heraldic laurel-wreath
design. It was largely because of the *Speedwell*'s moment in
wartime history that he'd decided to buy her.

Back here in town meanwhile, Eliot the scholarly slob
had started morphing back into Eliot the businessman.
For years his two selves had been intolerant of each other,

insisting that one life wasn't large enough for them both. He understood now that instead of tussling, each as with an unfriendly angel, they'd been edging for some time towards a truce. On his way that morning to the gathering at the Savoy, he'd spent a couple of hours in a quiet hotel restaurant in Bloomsbury where he and his new finance director had finalized the details of the company's retrenchment.

Most people, overhearing their conversation, would have found its bland technicalities dull enough for eyes to water and noses to run. For Eliot it was like being lifted free by a full tide; the more so for some details that hindsight made humiliatingly obvious. He should have promoted Elizabeth to this job years ago. Eliot had always noticed how little she spoke, but failed to appreciate how every word carried a payload of good sense, not to say on-the-nose special knowledge. He still didn't fancy her – thank God. But he began to see why her cerebral-looking husband might. With flooding relief he noted the contrast with Bernard, her predecessor, academically hyped yet reduced by the world of business to a chaotic funk.

Parts of his own workplace self had needed seeing off; that much he'd suspected for years. That headlong half-lunatic drive of youth – he couldn't have made his way without it, at first. But the habit of insecurity had rooted itself, then led him astray. It had been idiotic to take impossible loads of work home late each night, like a small child who won't part from its comfort blanket. And how had he come to believe, even unconsciously, that his business would be okay really, so long as he let it elbow the rest of life aside? When he came to putting it in order he'd been like the carpenter who can't stop to sharpen his saw, because his time is taken up by using a saw that's blunt.

One thing in particular was obvious. No way had this new self-knowledge faded up into view because of a mere few days off; not even as his first free time in years. At most the holiday had supplied the one missing glint of light, in itself scarcely visible, that subtly changes a wide panorama. Certainly he was damned if he'd go ahead now with selling the boat. If he had to, he'd drive the *Speedwell* to the cheapest canalside mooring he could find, and live in it on the rent from his house.

With his businessman self restored to purpose and good cheer, Eliot the scholar had also had a changed perspective. One he could scarcely wait to act upon…

*

In St Bartholomew the Great, Mike, musically subliterate, nonetheless half-recognized the introductory piece. A classical work that Jessie had always liked and had mastered rather well on the family piano as a teenager. It spoke of a spacious calm elation, in which spirit any tether to lesser things like hopes and fears was quite dissolved away. Such music came close as any to timelessness. Certainly it suited this place, even though the church, with its massy Romanesque pillars and mysterious perspectives, must have been nearly five hundred years old before the composer was born. Most City churches offered classical urbanity rather than medieval awe. Almost alone,

St Bartholomew's had survived both the Blitz and, by two short streets, the Great Fire, so that it now evoked the ghost of almost every ancient church which once stood within the city walls. Despite its size, the guests at Jessie and Ben's wedding nearly filled the nave, which an all-out spree of celebration had overflowed with swags and pedestals of white and yellow roses; Mike soon gave up on guessing how much the decorations had cost.

He'd assured himself he had to be here, if only on his own account. Making good. All down the river, starting with a whisper of disquiet, he'd known there was little time to be lost before he made direct contact with Sam and Jessie; yet each day he'd done nothing. Turning up here, uninvited but tactfully inconspicuous among so many people, would hardly be an ordeal. More like paying a small forfeit for not handing in an essay on time. Surely when they saw him sitting here, right at the back, almost out of earshot of the marriage vows, his children would forgive his brief failure to keep in touch.

Usually Mike was a very devil for punctuality, but somehow he'd arrived only just in time. One of the ushers, a young guy he didn't know, had showed him to what looked like the last free seat, on the aisle in the rearmost pew of the groom's side. From here he could stare all he liked, if only at a mass of back views. Pretending to make adjustments to where he sat, Mike stood up and took a better look. Anna was there at the front, hatless, in a familiar suit of raspberry-coloured raw silk that went with her dark auburn hair... Looking for their son, he realized Sam must be outside his line of sight, as best man. Once you allowed for how unlike their usual selves people were in wedding clothes, Mike thought he could recognize most of the congregation on Jessie's side of the church. Up at the front sat young Tom, Chris and Martha's lad, sporting a gold earring and a stumpy ponytail. Of course. He and Sam were close enough in age to be friends, having grown up as honorary cousins. Martha wasn't anywhere in sight, nor were Chris or Eliot; but then among themselves no one had actually mentioned today's ceremony.

However grand the setting, there was a feeling of sociability, shading to mateyness. People held murmured conversations over the back of their pew, or mimed a greeting across the nave. On either side of the altar steps a screen showed home movies from the couple's childhoods. Afterwards people from both sides of the congregation would remark how like each other the two video sequences had been. Each screen showed the holidays, on ski slopes, or terraces that bloomed with Mediterranean light; there were the birthday cakes, at first bigger than the child they celebrated; and later the spoofy graduation photos, with everyone so hairy they might almost have sported joke wigs. Several guests confided to each other how such similarity between the childhoods of bride and groom must surely be a good omen.

All Mike saw were the familiar images of his own family. How had he forgotten that a moving-picture show was now commonplace at weddings; that the years of shared life around Jessie's childhood would be raised up on high and beamed down at him with all of their images enlarged? Smiling and goofing around just for him presumably, back when he'd been the one behind the camera. Eliot was there, improbably younger, with their half-grown children both grubby, tousled and happy, burying him in a pile of grass scythed in their garden beneath the fruit trees. Elsewhere the infant Tom reached up, holding hands with Martha and Jessie as he learned to walk. He must have been filmed by Chris, from the look of adoration he directed at the camera.

Mike had forgotten too what a life of hospitality they'd led, in their own and their neighbours' pleasant suburban homes. How many such friends were here today? Already across the aisle he'd glimpsed the Goldblums, the Calders, and Maggie Zell's sharply dressed daughter, as shy in adulthood as when a child but earning silly money somewhere in EC4. He really must get in touch with more people; perhaps starting today, after the ceremony. The demands of his new family had been so overwhelming, he'd had no time to send out change-of-address cards ...even if they'd hadn't moved the houseboat to a new location. Maybe his own wedding this year shouldn't have been so modest; private, almost. But where would the money have come from, for a great cheerful splurge like this?

So thinking, he encountered a moment like a booby trap of iced water. From just across the nave the Calders had seen him; Debbie, in a small feathered hat worn slantwise, had even done a momentary double-take. Mike realised how he might look: skulking, so it must seem, in the pew furthest from his family. Perhaps they thought he'd be the one giving Jessie away. He raised his hand in greeting, with an expression of, yes: it is me. Having coolly returned his look to confirm that they'd recognised him, husband and wife made a point of turning away.

In many divorces, contested or not, there can be an element of vivisection. When the component parts of the marriage are shared out, bleeding or not, there's often one thing left that, unlike money or custody, doesn't concern the lawyers. No rules exist to say which partner gets the address file and the contact numbers, let alone the world's continuing goodwill.

Mike was lost to everything but this, when the images on the two screens froze and faded. The organist brought the overture to an end; and after a moment that rustled and vibrated with anticipation, he struck up a light-footed piece by Purcell, dignified and festive. On the arm of her uncle Angus, Jessie entered the church.

Mike hadn't realized how much, at that moment, he'd ache to see his daughter's face. But now that she was here he couldn't bring himself to risk meeting her eye. As if no other detail could interest him, he stared at the frothing white hem of her gown all the way up the nave.

The music ceased and the Very Reverend began his public greeting. Mike was at first too churned up to hear a thing. Only by degrees did he notice that whatever the man was saying he evidently had a senior cleric's equivalent of a good bedside manner; you couldn't miss his touch of informality, almost as if he were family. He recalled that Jessie had an occasional connection with this church, as a member of a well-respected choir made up of City workers.

Another hateful insight floated into his mind, as so

much dangerous loose debris. On the video loop he'd just been watching so intently, where had he himself appeared?

Nowhere, mate; you're invisible…

He hadn't always been the one behind the camera. In their photo albums, then the home movies, he'd been there in the frame as often as Anna, especially once the children had grown confident and wanted to try everything for themselves.

Such thoughts hassled him throughout the speech of welcome, then the first hymn. Sharing a hymnal with his neighbour, an elderly man he didn't know, he forced himself to lift up his head and sing loudly. His thoughts, whose marshalling and good order he usually took for granted, continued disorderly throughout the marriage ceremony itself, whose words would have been almost inaudible at this distance if they hadn't been so familiar. He wondered what sort of figure his ex-brother-in-law Angus was cutting; decent enough, no doubt. If he himself had been up there giving Jessie away, would he have been in full-dress uniform, medals included? He strove to shoo the image away; but once had, it was a thought that refused to be un-had.

'When in disgrace with Fortune and men's eyes
I all alone beweep my outcast state …'

A reading by someone from the same research team as Ben. With fierce, aimless purpose, Mike listened.

'…Yet in these thoughts myself almost despising
Haply I think on thee, and then my state
Like to the lark at break of day arising …'

So far today he'd surely done the right thing. It was tactful, so he insisted to himself, not to have looked straight at Jessie as she made her entrance. At such a moment, if he'd tried to make her acknowledge him she'd only have felt ambushed.

Another reading, from a woman he recognised as one of Anna's friends. Of course: aunt Isabel, Jessie's godmother.

'…To every thing there is a season … A time to weep and a time to laugh; a time to mourn and a time to dance … A time to get and a time to lose; a time to keep, and a time to cast away …'

What did this sonorous stuff mean? What the hell was it really about? It flickered through his mind that he'd briefly considered it for his own wedding, earlier this year … As part of a marriage service? How could he? With a scowl of concentration Mike took refuge in attending to the words of the service.

Between the readings were hymns, Jessie's taste prevailing. Old good tunes, to words in the muscular, easy language of the seventeenth century. Most of Jessie's preferences had centred on earlier stuff, by composers whose music sounded more impassioned for being restrained; not for her, anything too lush, uncorseted and nineteenth century.

'…Set me as a seal upon thine heart …for love is strong as death; jealousy is cruel as the grave: the coals thereof are coals of fire …Many waters cannot quench love, neither can the floods drown it …' A reading by Sam. Mike thought he looked older, as if his growing up had accelerated in the past few months. He could even imagine his son choosing these uncompromising words himself …

A Mozart overture accompanied the signing of the register; music to remind its hearers that though the angels might do serious overtime serenading God via other composers, it was proverbially Amadeus they went for in the stretches of eternity set aside for leisure.

Through all this, Mike's bearing could have been mistaken for prayer. Head lowered, he sat hunched up, his hands loosely clasped. Dismay had hold of him, as a dog shakes a rat.

But it was only dismay, not outright despair. He'd have lost touch with his very core of self if he hadn't held on to some grain of purpose. It would not do merely to come here, and be astonished by his own wretchedness, only to trail off home without exchanging a word or look with those he'd counted as his nearest. Let people say or do their worst. At least no one could count him a coward.

At the far end of the nave the bride and groom returned from the vestry. Amid another silence like a communal sigh of expectation, they turned to face west, ready to lead the procession from the church. A trumpeter, one of Jessie's friends from the Royal College of Music, sounded the opening from another classical piece, whose notes of triumph could stab you to the heart. Mike remembered to stand up like everyone else. He squared his shoulders.

Even now he couldn't look steadily at his daughter. He sneaked a glimpse while she and Ben were still some way off, the pair of them greeting people with an identical huge smile as they moved down the church towards him. Of course this was how they would look. So why should his own response surprise him? Why this sense of sudden danger? Bringing him close to tears?

Jessie's white presence passed from the edge of his sight. Her veil stirred and floated in the draught from the opened west door. Perhaps this was the moment when he gave up on will power and discipline, the so treacherous servants of his serial self-deceptions. All he cared about now, was how Anna would respond. Standing where he stood, resolutely gazing at her, he couldn't fail to be seen by her. He could do this. He'd always held fast under fire – even that time near Pristina when the man next to him had lost the top half of his head, not to a shell splinter but to flying debris, so bad had things been.

She was about to pass within half a yard of him.

In two paces their eyes would meet.

XXIX

There is properly no history, only biography.

History, Ralph Waldo Emerson (1803-82)

As London gathered around it and enlarged, the river had ceased to be a place of fantasy and frolicsome illusion. For Eliot the city was where loins got girded and decisions embraced. The *Speedwell* had embarked from her quiet mooring near Lechlade as the likely possession of a Siberian mining billionaire; today, had the deal gone through, Eliot would have sailed her back up river into Chelsea Harbour for a handover to agents of her new owner.

But on locking through from St Catherine's Dock into the Thames as if squeezed from a birth canal, without a thought he steered to port rather than starboard: not westward, back into the heart of the great city, but east, towards the estuary. The Russian deal was long since cancelled, even as he'd dwelt on other decisions. His resolve to sail down-river had been clinched that very morning by Marina's final call.

'My son has learned his lesson, I promise.'

'I'm glad for him.'

'I'll never have to pass on any money to him again. I'm absolutely sure of it.'

'That's a shame.'

'Eliot, don't try and confuse me. Please.'

'It means he'll miss out on the experience of learning his lesson again…and again…'

'Oh, I know you don't mean that really …'

'Shall we say, I think he's made a very promising career move. The purveyance of illegal pharmaceuticals may offer excellent prospects to someone of his qualities.'

'Oh, Eliot! I know you're not really making a joke of – of things.'

Don't you believe it, he thought.

He paused to savour the words in anticipation, then said, 'I'm going abroad for a while.'

'Oh, what fun! Where?'

'It's too soon to say,' he lied. 'But it does mean I won't be easy to reach.' Another whopper. But in Marina's case he was determined to make it come true.

He listened to her digesting this in silence, picturing her: the phone held a couple of inches away as if it suddenly needed cleaning; her mouth freeze-framed in a pout of surprise; and between her eyebrows an uncharacteristic crease. Marina rarely frowned, having trained herself not to for cosmetic reasons, whatever the provocation. Probably including nuclear strike.

Of course she knew what he really meant; she wasn't a complete idiot. To spare her from admitting that she understood, he spoke before she could.

'Goodbye Marina. Be fortunate.'

And rang off.

History can come for you, he thought, sailing now past receding shorelines towards the estuary and the sea. Mike, re-married, may have been shaken to the core, finding he'd staked everything on his so-called aspirant moment as a free spirit declaring for iconoclasm. And Chris? Probably wiser than he'd suspected, when he said history was a dangerous substance, to be handled with care the more you knew. What counted most, Chris had said, wasn't what you learned, whether consoling or dire, but what you did with it afterwards.

And what was wrong, Eliot wanted to know, with the use he himself had for history? Why deny him the side-effect of satisfaction he got from flushing out into history's gaze whatever heightened his personal sense of connection to the world? From looking backwards, the better to belong in his own time and place? Hence this new voyage, made as a scholar more than just a relative. Now that he was embarked, he couldn't believe the times he'd put off sailing to Deauville or St Malo, to start researching Edith's French period. The months she'd spent in Normandy had been the most productive of her short life, painting the hayfields, the depths of sun-flecked *bocages*, the old orchards of listing apple trees, the tall spindly poplars swagged with mistletoe, the cow-pastures udder-high in buttercups …There was no possible excuse for not going there. Particularly at this time of year.

The river widened to where it had a flat seaward horizon. The day was full of change, all fleeting shadows and glittering reaches pooled with light. Soon the

Speedwell would leave the Thames, which had borne so many invading fleets, sailed by men who stank of each other, and who ran about their rigging like an infestation or rowed in ranks to the beat of a drum.

Rounding Thanet and the North Foreland he passed the first point from which France could be seen: the chalky heights of Picardy, visible at this distance as a seeming chain of islands. West of the ship-swallowing Goodwin Sands, the waters held lapsed furrows turned by vessels recent enough to be part of his own life. Somewhere here the *Speedwell* was crossing her own former route, back from Dunkirk under a sky cross-hatched with trails left in combat and massively soiled by smoke from the bombed refineries on the French coast. Eliot had actually met one of the men her owner had rescued that day. As a cheerful elderly guy sitting in a pub near the Imperial War Museum he'd described his younger self making the voyage, a teenage squaddie half-mad with sleep starvation. His first encounter, safe on Kentish ground, had been with a young woman in Salvation Army uniform, dispensing hot drinks to rescued troops on the quayside at Ramsgate.

'She said to me, "Would you like a cup of tea?" I was only a lad and I started to cry … I should have married her.'

Out beyond the radio towers of Hellfire Corner and the white ferries sliding into Dover harbour, the *Speedwell* crossed another vanished trail, once carved in the sea by the boat on which Eliot, Mike and Chris had first met. Returning from Calais in bad weather, their ferry had approached Dover in such worsened conditions that it was found unsafe to attempt the harbour entrance. For over forty hours they'd had to ride out a storm that had sent every other passenger below with sea-sickness. Predicting no great loss from its open-handedness, for the rest of their time at sea the ferry company had offered to keep one bar open, with limitless free drinks.

A lilt of cheerfulness always accompanied Eliot's memory of how warily the three of them had sized each other up through the first couple of rounds.

Being of good heart and dwelling on his studies and his friends, he sailed blindly on, toward the past.